THE SHADOW MINISTER

LAURENCE RAPHAEL BROTHERS

THE SHADOW MINISTER

This is your narrator addressing you, my audience, directly. I mean this manuscript to come to the attention of foreign readers and so I shall intrude occasionally with footnotes or explanatory remarks in italics.

Lutèce was designed to be the ideal city, a metropolis of order and peace, prosperity and pleasure, magic, and romance. True, it wasn't entirely an original creation, and yet from the day of its founding to the present it has far surpassed the city from which its founder took inspiration, if I do say so myself.

My story concerns Jules Janvier more than anyone else. He's one of Lutèce's exceedingly rare magically disabled individuals, but please, don't pity him for being immune to healing magic or being unable to light his pipe with a snap of his fingers. He'd hate that. Janvier is an earnest young man, age 24, which made him the youngest commissaire in the history of the Police Judiciaire by some 15 years. Coming out of school, he had expected to use his social work degree to forward a career in the beloved Patrouille Communautaire branch of the police (nine times larger than the Police Judiciaire), helping neighborhood people get through life's little difficulties.

More about what propelled Janvier into his role as head of the Serious Crimes squad will come later, but for now we'll pick him up as he pays his respects to Baron Corbeau, reclusive nobleman and art collector.

It's Monday, May 23rd, in Lutèce's 532nd year Après-Palimpseste, a warm sunny day.

1

COMMISSAIRE JANVIER LOOKED at the calling card he'd been handed. No text, just a blue cat printed on fancy white cardstock. The cat seemed to be stalking disdainfully away into the depths of the card, its tail upraised to reveal a little white asterisk of an asshole. Janvier suppressed his smile; he didn't want to give Baron Corbeau the impression an imminent theft from his collection was a joking matter.

"I found this … card on my secretaire early this morning," the baron said, gesturing at a small antique desk full of pigeonholes and tiny drawers. "I suppose it must be a … declaration of a burglary to come."

The elderly Baron Corbeau bore a passing resemblance to his namesake raven, with a long black frockcoat and sparse combed-over black hair for plumage and a harsh rasping voice for a caw. He was tall and thin to the point of gauntness, with curious vertical lines in his long, pallid face and a thick convex monocle clenched in his right eye.

Janvier, heavy-set and brown-haired, was addressing Baron Corbeau in the collector's cluttered, claustrophobic office. The interview was taking place atop the baron's ancestral Tour des Corbeaux, a black basalt tooth of a tower that sprouted like an invasive plant in the middle of Lutèce's otherwise modern and fashionable 9th arrondissement. The baron had walked rapidly up eight flights of stairs without showing any sign of fatigue.

Commissaire Janvier was grateful to be able to take a few moments to study the card and catch his breath before answering, turning it over to look at the blank white reverse and running his finger over the faint impressions left by the rotogravure press as if they held some secret meaning.

"Indeed, Monsieur," Janvier said at last, "It appears you have been targeted by the notorious thief who calls themself le Chat Azur."

"I ... see ..."

Janvier was beginning to dislike the baron purely on the basis of his ellipses, which he dragged out interminably.

"Is there any piece in particular you think they're after?"

The baron shook his head. "None...in particular. You are welcome to survey...my collection, however."

Janvier sighed. Still, it was necessary to maintain an air of professionalism. Baron Corbeau was wealthy and politically connected. Inspecteur-general Lambert, Janvier's boss and the chief of Criminal Investigations, had made it clear to him in this morning's staff meeting that he must handle the nobleman's concerns with kid gloves.

At length, waiting impatiently through the ellipses, Janvier learned the basic facts of the situation. In order to deliver their brazen calling-card, the thief had presumably crept right past the baron's bedroom next door while he was sleeping. The tower's entry doors were kept locked and unfriendly-looking iron bars blocked the windows, unusual measures in a city in which ordinary citizens never had to worry about a break-in.

"Very well, Monsieur," Janvier said. "Two patrol officers from the 9th arrondissement will be stationed outside the

Tour des Corbeaux at all times starting this afternoon. An inspector will be present in your gallery until either the thief is apprehended or ... well ...”

Baron Corbeau grinned without humor; on seeing his bared teeth, Janvier became uncomfortably aware of the bones beneath the art collector's skin. He suffered a shocking hallucination: the flesh of the baron's face melted to reveal a naked, leering skull beneath. Janvier shuddered and looked hastily away; it was an intrusive phantasm of the kind he had learned to suppress over the last two years.

“You were going to say ... until the theft actually takes place?”

Janvier looked up. The skull was gone. The baron appeared normal again. But Janvier's heart was still racing and he felt sweat beading out on his forehead. He had to make an effort to answer in a calm tone of voice.

“We will take every precaution, Monsieur.”

•   •   •

Leaving the Tour des Corbeaux, still upset from the hallucinatory episode, Janvier was struck once again how out of place the building looked in the heart of the bustling 9th arrondissement, a baleful black tower stuck in the middle of a neighborhood of familiar six-story apartment buildings, none more than a century old. He took the electric tram across town to police headquarters, pleased for once with the crowd on board and the loud clickety-clack of the wheels rattling over the rails. The creepy old tower and its even creepier owner had induced a morbid feeling which combined with that horrible hallucination had made Janvier extremely anxious and tense. Back in the everyday world he felt much better.

•   •   •

Janvier crossed the street from the tram stop, and as always, he paused at the door to police headquarters, #36

Quai des Serpents, an old stone pile that abutted the city's central court building. Even after two years he couldn't quite believe he was working here, not just as a criminal investigator but as a commissaire. The court and police HQ took up a substantial part of the western part of the Ile des Serpents, an elongated island on the Rivière Serpentine whose coils cut the city in half.

After ascending a flight of well-worn stairs, Janvier stopped at the detectives' staff room. The two inspectors on Janvier's team were in the room chatting with officers from other squads, plainly waiting for his return, so he knocked on the open door and when they looked up, he gestured for them to accompany him to his office.

Janvier's dark, cramped office was in an out of the way corner of the floor. As a commissaire promoted to a newly created position, a place had to be found for him but it was far from luxurious. His two subordinates filled all the available space in the little office; the senior inspector, Jeanne-Marie de l'Épée, had the visitor chair to Janvier's left, while the junior, Richard Frémont, stood in the corner on other side where he would be sure to be bashed by the door if someone opened it without knocking.

The one advantage of the tiny room, its walls packed with ancient wooden filing cabinets and its interior almost entirely taken up by Janvier's equally old and scarred desk, was a view of the river winding close by, almost under his window. When he had nothing better to do, Janvier found it relaxing to let his gaze wander out over the water, observing the doings of the goods barges and pleasure craft. On the Ile de Lutèce, a long slender island downriver, he could just see the central dome of the royal palace where the not-quite-entirely-powerless Queen Francoise IV might well be sitting down to an afternoon breakfast with whichever courtesan was her current favorite.

Before speaking, Janvier selected a pipe from the rack on his desk, and once it was tamped down to his satisfaction, lit the tobacco with a chemical match from the box in his top drawer. By now, neither of his inspectors saw anything odd about him using the match instead of simply conjuring a sorcerous flame like any other citizen would do. They knew Janvier was one of the rare disabled people who couldn't cast even simple household spells. His pipe drawing well at last, Janvier explained Baron Corbeau's situation to Frémont and de l'Épée and let them examine le Chat Azur's calling card.

"It's our job to stop the blue cat!" Frémont exclaimed. "This should be fun."

"Not as fun as you might think," Janvier said. "I'm afraid we're going to have to work the tower interior ourselves. And that means eight-hour shifts with nothing much to do but look solemn. Which times do you fancy? Morning or evening? I'll take the graveyard shift myself."

Frémont, a blond, fresh-faced junior inspector two years younger than Janvier, clearly had a preference, but he hesitated, allowing his senior to speak first. The gray-haired de l'Épée smiled at his deference.

De l'Épée, an athletic woman in her mid 50s, was in rich brown herringbone tweed today, the fabric imported from the remote semi-barbarian nation of Albion. Frémont favored a violet serge from an Esperian designer that Janvier secretly envied. As a commissaire, he'd been restricting himself to staid grays and muted pinstripes in his suits; the colorful blazers and dashing capes he'd been fond of at university moldered in the back of his wardrobe. Today, Janvier wore a subfusc wool suit with a dull maroon tie.

"Go on, Richard," de l'Épée said. "It makes no difference to me."

"In that case, the morning shift, please. But I'm always at your service, Chief, at any hour of the day or night."

Frémont sometimes made Janvier just a bit uncomfortable, as the inspector regarded him with a degree of admiration he was sure he didn't merit; Janvier also suspected him of harboring some secret fantasies of romance, which wouldn't have been a problem if they hadn't been superior and subordinate. Frémont was an enthusiastic clubgoer, he'd probably requested the morning shift so he'd be free for recreation in the evening.

"Duly noted. I'll take over from you at ten o'clock at night, Jeanne-Marie. Richard, you'll have to be at the Tour des Corbeaux at six tomorrow morning. It's going to be tedious work. If we had more people, I'd make it four-hour shifts or at least put you in teams, but so it goes. You mustn't let the baron catch you napping."

"Understood." De l'Épée rose from her chair. "I should set off at once for my shift."

"No hurry this first day," Janvier said. "Since they left their calling-card just last night, the thief is hardly likely to strike immediately. For style points they'll want to let us set up properly before executing their theft. So, let's take a minute or two to discuss the case, shall we?"

De l'Épée sat back down. "Of course, sir."

"According to our colleagues in Art Crimes who have so kindly handed us this thankless job, Baron Corbeau doesn't actually have anything in his collection that combines the chic allure and high price that attracts the top League thieves. There's something fishy about this to begin with. Keep your eyes open in case we're being misdirected."

"Will do, Chief."

After further discussion of the notorious thief's past exploits and futile speculation what they might be after this time, Janvier waved his inspectors out. As an envoi he added, "Next up for me is the lab, in the unlikely event Dr. Bernard can make something out of this calling-card."

•   •   •

Janvier's visit to the police forensic laboratory was fruitless, as expected. The card provided no clues. Since the use of calling-cards to announce a theft was the hallmark of the Ligue des Voleurs, it would be pointless to survey print shops for its origin; the card had certainly been produced by the League's own printer, a shop whose staff had steadfastly resisted every form of pressure the police had been able to bring to bear.

•　　　•　　　•

A word about the Ligue des Voleurs: Lutèce was noteworthy compared to the city of my birth for its almost complete lack of malicious crime. The occasional drunken brawl might arise on Friday and Saturday nights, but rarely anything more serious than that. Even crimes of passion were all but unknown. Ordinary citizens never had to lock their doors because no one was needy enough to steal. Theft was rather the province of the sporting amateurs of the League.

The rules of their game had been laid down long ago during the reign of their patron and sponsor, Queen Françoise I. Violence was absolutely forbidden as was wanton property damage, and the only allowed targets were the unique treasures of the ultra-rich who could easily afford their losses. Perhaps in recognition of the unmalicious nature of these crimes, the statute of limitation on art theft was only a year after which the thief could parade their acquisition publicly or sell it back to its owner as the case might be. Of course, if they were caught in the act or during the statute period with stolen art in their possession the thieves faced prison time, but that was the risk of the game. Though technically the entire League was guilty of criminal conspiracy, long precedent protected League officials and staff from police harassment.

•　　　•　　　•

Janvier returned to his office to flip through the slender file he'd obtained from Commissaire Renard of the Art Crimes squad, the most prestigious department of Criminal Investigations. Le Chat Azur had appeared on the scene just a few years ago, first making headlines by stealing the Étoile Noire diamond, the centerpiece of the crown jewels, from its secure viewing chamber in the Musée Royal. Since then, they'd scored triumphs with the thefts of Conti's Portrait of Chevaliere d'Armagnac, a recent impressionist painting deemed a masterpiece by the judges of the Academy; the notorious Orgy Triptych by Dupont which illustrated every sexual combination, position, and kink known to humanity with meticulous, loving care; and their crowning achievement to date, the burglary of La Comtesse Souriante from the Musée National. La Comtesse was the supreme artistic work of the pre-Palimpsest era, a painting whose majesty was enough to overcome its lack of attributed artist, history, or provenance. One night the painting vanished, replaced by a pastiche on the original. The replacement was popularly acclaimed as being superior due to its content, even though inferior in actual artistry: La Comtesse en Rémanence depicted the same subject as a plainly postcoital nude.

Together these marvelous crimes were enough to propel le Chat Azur into the top ranks of the League of Thieves in record time. Through the usual League intermediaries, the thief had sold most of the stolen items back to their owners or to the insurance company as soon as the statute of limitations expired, but the Orgy Triptych was apparently still in their possession. In a show of good humor from the curators of the Musée National, the two Comtesses were now displayed side by side.

Janvier had no doubt that the thief's cleverness would overcome whatever dull defenses he could prepare. At least he might perhaps have the privilege of being the first to figure out how they'd done it, whatever the theft was going to be.

He stopped at his neighborhood épicerie on the way home so he could pick up some caffeinated cola water and a package of candy to tide him over during the tedious watch hours he expected that night. Any other inspector would be able to cast wakefulness spells as needed, but Janvier couldn't even ask a pharmacist to cast one for him, as a side-effect of his disability made him resistant to most spell effects. He'd be smoking his pipe too, of course, but this was a new vice for Janvier and too much smoke made his mouth dry out.

2

A T LAST, WE COME TO A PAUSE *convenient to describe Janvier's peculiar disability as well as the circumstances surrounding his unprecedented promotion.*

Extensive testing at the university had revealed that the capacity most people had for deliberate spellcasting in him seemed to be working in reverse, as if he were always unconsciously casting an antimagic spell. This interfered with his life in a thousand minor ways, from having to light fires with matches to being the sole person at the picnic plagued by mosquitoes to having to hang his laundry out to dry rather than simply banishing its moisture. He couldn't use cosmetic spells at all, and so he often came off as a bit more unkempt than his peers. But apart from these minor annoyances, his disability also had larger and more serious consequences. His lovemaking was affected as he had to wear a condom with a woman to avoid pregnancy; his condition would even interfere with a partner's contraceptive spells. Perhaps the worst impact was on Janvier's health. In the event of a serious injury, a broken bone or the trauma of a major wound, what would take anyone else a day or two to heal with sorcerous assistance would be weeks or months for him. Janvier knew that later in life he'd be subject to all manner of infirmities of aging that other citizens didn't experience, and he'd come to accept that he was unlikely to reach the usual centenarian lifespan.

On the other hand, it wasn't all bad. As a junior officer in the Patrouille Communautaire, Janvier would never have apprehended the Butcher of Mars if he weren't disabled in this particular way, as the murderer's powerful illusion spells had failed to work on him. He'd seen the deranged shopkeeper, Lutèce's only serial killer in over 500 years of recorded history, walking home through crowds of civilians who seemed strangely disinterested in his blood-stained garments or the dripping cleaver in his hands. Janvier, then attached to the 18th arrondissement, followed him to his flat on the first floor above his quaint little butcher shop on the Butte de Mars where the gruesome trophies he'd cut from his victims were up on shelves.

As a result of his success, bringing relief to a city traumatized by horror, a police force whose reputation had plummeted, and a government on the verge of being forced to resign, Janvier was cosseted, awarded, transferred to the Police Judiciaire, and promoted three grades to the coveted position of commissaire of the newly created Serious Crimes squad. But he suffered from nightmares thereafter along with intrusive thoughts and monstrous images during the day, and though therapy eased the worst of these symptoms, from time to time he underwent a renewed onslaught.

Now, back to our earnest commissaire.

•   •   •

Janvier opened the front door of his apartment building. Maître Bouchard bustled out of his ground-floor lodge to meet Janvier in the entry foyer, a spotless black-and-white tiled hall. Bouchard was an apple-cheeked white-haired gentleman who continued to wear the tight leather trousers he'd favored as a young man. They still looked good on him, too. The former courtesan, a maître émérite of the Guilde du Plaisir[1], now served as the building concierge, a traditional Lutèce occupation for retirees who wanted to keep busy.

"Commissaire!" Bouchard called out, "You have a special delivery!"

"Really?"

The concierge held out an envelope. "This came by courier an hour ago. Not through the post. Is it connected to a case?"

To Janvier's embarrassment, the concierge had treated him like a hero for the last two years and showed no signs of letting up. The envelope he handed over was one of those complicated folded things, not sealed with glue or tape, and it took Janvier a minute to work out how to undo it. But based on the size and the feel of what it contained, he'd already guessed—Yes. Another of le Chat Azur's calling cards. Blank, with no message.

Janvier knew that Bouchard must be eager to find out what it was. He couldn't think of any good reason to hold it back so he handed him the card.

"My first brush with such a notorious celebrity," Janvier said.

"Is this—le Chat Azur! Oh! Are you in a detective-vs-thief duel with them? I'm so excited!"

Janvier laughed. "It better not be a duel. I can't possibly win. All I can really hope is to be an admiring bystander to their brilliance."

"Don't talk like that! I'm sure you'll make the arrest!"

"We'll see," Janvier said. "But I'm afraid you'll read the headline in a few days, 'The Azure Cat Strikes Again!' And below in smaller print, 'Janvier Baffled, Admits Defeat.'"

---

[1] The two most respected professions in Lutèce were courtesan and healer, both with their own special programs of undergraduate and graduate study at the university. For obvious reasons the introductory courtesan courses were very popular electives, but many conscientious students learned at least the basics of healing magic as well.

Bouchard snorted. "I don't think so. But Commissaire, when you make the arrest ..."

"Get you an autograph? But of course."

Like many in the city, Bouchard was a fan of the League of Thieves. Unfortunately, he knew no more of le Chat Azur than anyone else; the thief had done an excellent job of keeping themself mysterious even to the tenacious reporters of the city's tabloids. At length, Janvier detached himself from Bouchard's eager speculations and went upstairs to his modest one-bedroom flat with its heavy old oaken furniture inherited from a previous tenant. Apart from a bookcase of novels and criminology texts in the salon and a large succulent overflowing its pot in his bedroom, he'd hardly given the place any personal touch at all.

Janvier prepared a quick, light dinner, Esperian-style cacio e pepe spaghetti with an asparagus vinaigrette on the side. Of course, he had to use a match to light the gas range. He dined on his balcony with a bottle of the cheap, bitter vin de table from the Bois Perdus that he'd learned to like as a student.

As he ate, he flipped through a volume of stories about Le Fantôme Pâle, a fictional thief whose exploits he'd adored as a child. He was fascinated by the diverse sleights the author deployed, the fiendish disguises, the concealment of a supposedly stolen item in plain sight at the scene, the replacement of a stolen gem with a facsimile, the clever uses of old spells in new ways, and all kinds of novel mechanical tricks: clockwork timers, mirrors, magic lanterns, networks of combustible silk threads, a whole world of innovative techniques that would never have occurred to Janvier on his own.

Using the telephone always felt like an exciting adventure; Janvier had moved to the head of the five-year waiting list for new line installation as a result of his promotion and had placed his first personal call just last year. He checked in at the Quai des Serpents to see if anyone had left a message for him with the switchboard. Nothing. At least that meant the thief hadn't already struck; it would have been embarrassing if they had after he'd dismissed the idea earlier. Janvier puttered around his flat until he couldn't stand it anymore, and at last it was time to set out for the Tour des Corbeaux to relieve de l'Épée.

The trams stopped running at 8:00 PM on Monday nights and tricycle cabs were rare in his neighborhood at this hour, so Janvier had to use his phone to call an electric cab to get to the baron's tower. Though it was amusing to ride in the rickety humming contraption, something he never did on his own time, he didn't look forward to the expense report; his charges were examined meticulously by the interior ministry bookkeepers responsible for paying police bills.

Despite Lutèce's well-lit gas-lamp thoroughfares (renowned worldwide as the city of light) the Tour des Corbeaux was dark and gloomy when Janvier pulled up in his cab. The tower's black stone seemed to suck up all ambient light. It was surrounded by shadow on all sides apart from the lamplit front door. Standing in its own little plaza isolated from any neighbor, the tower had no grounds or garden; its peculiar nonagonal spire ascended 35 meters into the air, the smooth, sheer sides of the cyclopean structure unbroken by beam ends or other handholds save for the barred windows.

•　　　•　　　•

The tower's presence in Lutèce was contrary to my plans for the city, but early on I found that a few such expressions of antiquity were beyond my power to eradicate. I really should have investigated this more deeply when I had the chance, but I assumed it was a random quirk of the Instrumentality I'd inherited, not the hallmark of something much more dire. Until just prior to the events of this narrative, when a certain interest was aroused, the place meant little more to me than a memento of a lost world.

•　　　•　　　•

The Tour des Corbeaux looked impossible to climb without hammering spikes into the stone; a rope might be lowered by a confederate from a window and the bars removed with some effort using heavy tools, but then the question was how the confederate managed to get in. Anyway, even the most athletic climber would be exposed on the wall for at least a minute, not even counting the considerable time required to remove the bars.

The tallest nearby buildings were the usual six-story types much like Janvier's own block of flats. From the roof of one of those buildings, the nearest 50 meters distant, a line might conceivably be strung to one of the tower's middle-story windows (or less easily all the way up to the tower's roof, which had a rounded cornice unsuitable for a grapnel). Janvier couldn't see how even a magically strengthened silk line could plausibly be secured to the tower in the first place, however. The tower's stone would hardly allow a crossbow's bolt drawing a line behind it to sink in, and though a grapnel could perhaps hook on a sill or a window bar, 50 meters was a long way to throw one. Even if it could be done, surely it would take several loud, clanging attempts before the grapnel would hook on, having to be reeled back repeatedly right through the street below, and then the thief would have to traverse the line, exposed to view from the Boulevard des Oliviers. Magic could aid stealth, suppress sounds and amplify darkness, but true invisibility was unknown.

Putting such forms of entry aside, what else remained? The front door? With patrol officers standing right there? No. Of course, there might be a distraction that would draw the officers away, but even then … no. Far too risky. A hydrogen balloon painted black for stealth against the night sky, with a daring thief performing a rappelling descent to the roof? Ridiculous. It was impossible to control a balloon's flight so precisely, even if somehow one could be lofted in secret without the whole city knowing it.

That left two other methods the thief might employ. The first had to do with securing legitimate access to the tower, perhaps in the guise of a servant, since Baron Corbeau wasn't likely to host any parties or invite guests now that he had been warned a theft was imminent. Le Chat Azur might have found employment in advance, or bribed an existing servant not to appear, showing up in their place under a disguise spell. It should be easy enough to check that last out, as such spells would unravel in Janvier's immediate presence.

Another very slight chance involved the subornation or replacement of the patrol officers from the 9th's station. But on reflection, Janvier decided to rule that out because he didn't want to seriously consider the possibility of such treason. He would never have succumbed to blandishment or bribery when he was a patrol officer, and he couldn't imagine any of his former colleagues doing so either. Even for a crime with so little moral significance as a League art theft. And entering through the front door was fraught with peril anyway, because le Chat Azur couldn't know if there was someone waiting inside.

A final possibility from his story collection occurred to Janvier: a secret entrance. The tower was too isolated for above-ground access to make sense, but everyone knew that Lutèce was riddled with old limestone and gypsum mine workings, not to mention a famous cavern system in the 5th and 6th arrondissements, so it wasn't impossible the tower had some underground access. Janvier had never heard of anything like that here in the 9th, but he knew that some old shafts had been tunneled deep into the Butte de Mars next door in the 18th, and some of those connected to people's basements.

Janvier clambered out of the cab, paid off the driver and secured a receipt, then walked across the plaza to the tower's front door. The police officer there was familiar to him though he only knew his nickname: Sandy, a walrus-mustached veteran who couldn't possibly be a thief or a thief's confederate for that matter.

"Commissaire." The officer saluted punctiliously. "All's well. Nothing to report on my shift."

"Good. Where's your colleague?"

"My inspector decided to station her at a vacant flat across the street that has good sight lines on the plaza. We trade off every two hours."

"Excellent. Carry on, then."

Janvier rang the bell and a minute later de l'Épée opened the front door. She looked as alert and put together as if this was the beginning of her day, not the end of a long tedious shift.

"Welcome, chief. Nothing's happened all day. Shall I show you around?"

"Please do. I only went straight up to the Baron's office this morning, and I was out of breath most of the way."

De l'Épée chuckled. "I can believe it. I've been getting my exercise, too. The collection covers three of the nine floors, but at least they're contiguous ones, five through seven."

They walked through a small entry foyer with a cloakroom on one side and a closet on the other to get to a fancy hall with a double-height ceiling. The hall featured polished squares of cream and pink marble on the floor and an oil-lamp chandelier glittering with quartz crystal pendants.

Two doors were present here at floor level on the left and right sides of the far wall. Grand curving stairways further to either side led up to a gallery level that overlooked the hall with double doors in the center of the gallery corridor, opposite the foyer.

"Kitchen and larder and a laundry room down here past the left door. A drawing room and lavatory to the right. Up the stairs is a formal dining room connected by dumbwaiter to the kitchen and also the start of the stairs you must have taken to get to the top this morning. It doesn't double back; on each story the flight moves another angle of the nine walls around to the left. Do you want to look at any of the rooms down here?"

"Just the kitchen and the larder."

De l'Épée raised an eyebrow but didn't ask him why. Of course, Janvier expected to find access to a wine cellar through one of these rooms. They entered an enormous kitchen replete with the usual stoves, ovens, sinks, and countertops. Pots and pans hung from hooks on the walls, and a wooden rack featured two dozen knives of all sizes and shapes. It didn't look like most of the items got a lot of use, however.

"I don't think he entertains much," de l'Épée said. She pointed out the dumbwaiter, which Janvier checked to make sure it wasn't connected to a hidden basement, and they passed through another door from the kitchen into a well-stocked larder with two small wooden doors on the far wall. "Cold room through the left door. Standard enchantment. Meat and dairy and so on."

Janvier didn't have a refrigerator of his own because he'd ruin the spell whenever he opened the door, so he only ever bought just enough perishable food to prepare the same day.

"The other door goes to the wine cellar?"

"Right," said de l'Épée. "I looked down there briefly just for completeness' sake. One room, old and dusty. The servants don't clean it. Lots of bottles, a thousand at least. Probably most of them have gone off, however. A pity."

Janvier asked, "What are your thoughts about techniques that le Chat Azur might use?"

"All my ideas seem too risky. I can't see a top-notch thief trying to climb the wall under surveillance, prying the bars off the windows, or picking the lock on the front door. The baron only has daytime staff from a service, no permanent servants. Anyway, he's just suspended the service for the week, so it's not going to be an inside job, either."

"Really? No secretary? No valet?"

"No one at all, and no relatives, either. Confirmed bachelor. He'll be cooking for himself or dining out, I suppose. Right now, he's up in his office doing I don't know what just as he has been all day. Apart from the officer out front you and I are the only other people in the whole tower."

"Hm."

They ascended the grand stairway to the gallery that looked out over the ground floor foyer. The ornately appointed formal dining room behind a pair of double doors was clean, but it gave off an air of disuse, nevertheless.

"The rest of the tower has the same layout as this floor," de l'Épée said, as they walked up the next flight of stairs to the second story. "See, here's the landing. It opens into a central room, and from the center you can get to eight rooms up against the walls as the ninth wall has the stairs. Three floors with just one guard may be a bit chancy, but I still don't see how le Chat Azur even gets inside."

"Ha, ha!" Janvier gestured grandly, like a stage magician revealing a miracle. "Unless ... *the thief is already here!*"

"What? Wait, you don't mean—" de l'Épée's mouth opened in an "O" of astonishment.

He regretted his flamboyance at once. "I don't! I don't mean anything! It's just I've been reading some heist stories as preparation for the job, and in the stories the thief always challenges the detective's most basic assumptions about what's going on."

"Oh. I was hoping for a brilliant deduction."

"Not from me," Janvier said, smiling. "But I really should have asked if you've worked any League jobs before."

De l'Épée smiled in turn and shook her head. "I'm afraid not. I was never in Art Crimes, and they're usually quite protective of their territory."

"Which leads to the question: why us, this time? But I suppose we can put that off for the moment. Let's finish touring the tower."

•   •   •

"What a mess," Janvier said. They were in a cluttered little chamber on the fourth floor. Like most of the other rooms on the lower levels, it was crammed full of obscure antiques and curios. This room featured items in bell jars: mangy stuffed animals, dried flower arrangements, old ormolu clocks, miniature orreries, intricate doll houses, and other even more recondite items.

He shook his head. "Since Art Crimes thinks Baron Corbeau's actual collection is nothing much, I was wondering if perhaps one of these curios might have special value known to the thief but not to the baron. But this is really too much. We'd never be able to sort through all this ... stuff."

"It would be impossible," said de l'Épée. "You asked me to look for special works among the paintings we'll see starting on the next floor, but I really couldn't find anything notable. It's mostly what the art history scholars call expressionism with a bit of something even stranger called cubism. Neither mode has been in fashion since the Palimpsest era. I rather like some of it, but nothing stood out for me. Without any signature or provenance, a pre-Palimpsest work has to be truly amazing to be worth a thief's time. Like La Comtesse en—La Comtesse Souriante, I mean."

"You seem quite knowledgeable," Janvier said. "I'm impressed."

"It's superficial. My wife drags me to the Musée National every so often in the fond hope some culture will sink in. It hasn't so far. But after you dismissed us yesterday, I conferred briefly with one of the Art Crimes inspectors, who gave me a quick introduction to art collecting from a thief's point of view."

"Oh, well. I should take a turn through the gallery, even so. Point out your favorite, at least."

"I can do that. I like the ultramarines on the fifth floor."

The art on the three gallery floors of the tower mostly left Janvier unmoved, as expected, but then fine art wasn't really his thing anyway. His favorites were a group of paintings of elegant, arch-looking women with sharp, unrealistically angular features that all must have been daubed by the same artist, though of course the signatures had been erased during the Palimpsest Event[2].

---

[2] This is really too involved for a footnote, so I'll explain it to foreign readers at greater length when the opportunity arises for a pause.

At last, de l'Épée and Janvier finished their tour of the tower, apart from the top floor which the baron had asked them to avoid except in an emergency. Janvier did climb the ladder from the top-floor landing up to the roof to get a feel for its situation, trying to move quietly so as not to provoke the baron's reprimand if he were still awake.

Standing on the flat rooftop, a stiff breeze blowing past him, Janvier briefly entertained his balloon fantasy. He imagined a great black gasbag passing overhead, its bulk blocking out the stars, the thief descending lightly by rope … It seemed sillier than ever now that he was actually up here.

Anyway, the tower's height provided a lovely view of Lutèce's right bank. To the north the dark bulk of the Butte de Mars in the 18th arrondissement rose with its quaint village-like community, no doubt all asleep in their beds. Janvier knew the streets there very well, but even though he lived not far from the foot of the hill he hadn't visited the summit in the two years since he'd arrested the Butcher of Mars in his little house near the very top of the butte. Just to the south, the neighborhood around the Place des Lutins was brilliant with clubs, theaters, bars, and restaurants.

Somewhat further south, the Lutins entertainment district gave way to a fancy commercial zone, its streets still lit despite the stores being closed at this hour, and off in the distance Janvier could see the Opéra National, illuminated by ultra-expensive electric-arc floodlights that caused the sky above the building to glow. Further off still the dark coils of the Serpentine river bisected the city; with a telescope Janvier was sure he could have made out police headquarters, though unfortunately his office window faced south rather than north, and so he wouldn't be able to see himself there, working late. Frowning a little at the whimsical thought, Janvier descended to the eighth floor, making sure the trapdoor to the roof was secured behind him. Just in case he was wrong about the balloon.

After escorting de l'Épée to the front door and locking it with the huge old-fashioned key she'd handed him, Janvier walked downstairs to check out the wine cellar.

As de l'Épée had said, the cellar wasn't big enough to hide anything, being just fifteen meters across. Old, dusty racks lined the walls, with other racks projecting out into the room's center to add storage space. It didn't look promising for any sort of hidden entrance, but just for completeness Janvier circled the room rapping on the wooden shelving in case one concealed the hollow space of a tunnel behind it. They all sounded the same. The floor was dry packed earth that showed no hint of having been disturbed for decades. Oh well: so much for that bright idea.

Annoyed at having wasted his time, Janvier paused, curious about the wine that looked to have been left undisturbed for generations. He pulled out a cobwebby old bottle at random, brushed it off, and found it had a paper label, completely blank except for the printed image of a greyhound, the ink of the lines faded to a wispy pale brown.

•　　•　　•

Aha. Now's the time for my deferred explanation. The Palimpsest Event was the abiding mystery of Lutèce's history (and indeed of the world's history) which only went back 532 years even though it was plain to historians that the world in pretty much its current form must have existed for far longer. In the moment of the Palimpsest Event, all writing, whether ink on paper, oil on canvas, carved in stone, or even tattooed on skin, had been erased everywhere in the world. With this great erasure, all detailed knowledge of past generations had been lost.

It was unclear to modern historians why this inexplicable event, completely beyond the scope of any known sorcery, hadn't generated civil disorder or at least widespread unrest, and why there hadn't been enormous amounts of writing about the event and about recent memories generated immediately thereafter. In fact, it had taken a whole generation before anyone started to speculate about what had happened, and investigation into the mystery (uniformly futile) had only really kicked off in the following century after all the survivors of the event had died.

•   •   •

Janvier replaced the bottle in its rack. All the pre-Palimpsest wine in the cellar must have turned to vinegar and mud by now, but suppose there were bottles of port or brandy that had managed to survive the centuries? What might they be worth? Janvier had no idea, but they would certainly be novelties, possibly alluring enough to a League thief to make a worthwhile target. He'd never heard of any wine or spirits that old appearing on the market.

But even if this speculation was on target, it still didn't address how le Chat Azur was planning to get into the tower in the first place. Janvier thought the balance of probability was still with an artwork theft, so he trudged back up the stairs to the gallery levels.

When he stepped onto the sixth story landing, the little pocket watch dangling from his fob emitted a muted chime. It was precisely ten o'clock.

3

B Y 10:30, THE BARON'S GALLERY had lost any appeal of novelty it might once have had. Janvier had plodded heavily up and down the stairs and walked past each of the hundred and sixty-seven paintings before returning to his starting point on the sixth floor.

By 11:00 (his watch chimed), he was calculating how long his raspberry pastilles would last him; the tin had twenty pastilles and he'd already eaten three.

By 11:30, Janvier hadn't eaten a pastille for 32 minutes and was thinking how ridiculous it was to have stopped merely because he was embarrassed to have calculated his consumption rate. He looked longingly at the stairway that he could use any time he liked to climb down to the front door to chat with the officer on duty or even to nip off to a bistro for refreshments. He *was* a commissaire, after all. There were only twelve in the whole country, and only four higher ranking police officers. He could do what he wanted short of flagrant disobedience to orders. But he didn't move. It seemed like shirking somehow.

By 11:55, Janvier was angry at Baron Corbeau for provoking the attentions of a League thief, at his boss, the stodgy Inspecteur-general Lambert for seconding him to this stupid duty, and at the suave, elegant Commissaire Renault of Art Crimes for requesting his assistance in the first place.

The final five minutes of the day seemed like an eternity. Midnight was a meaningless point in time with six hours left in a seemingly infinite watch but Janvier looked forward to it as a moment in which he would settle down to an eventless night of drudgery. Knowing that the hour had no significance he deliberately didn't look at his watch, and so the chime took him by surprise. At that instant the whole atmosphere of the tower changed, or at least it seemed to, becoming colder, darker, and more ominous.

Janvier wiped his brow. He knew this creepy feeling was just his imagination, more nastiness tossed up by his subconscious. He pulled a bottle of RV Cola (Réveillez-vous, Monsieur! Réveillez-vous, Madame!) out of his pocket and used the bottle opener on his keychain to pop the cap.

"I hope you brought enough to share." The voice came from behind him. He whipped around ... no one was there.

When Janvier turned back she was standing right there, a tall figure dressed in skin-tight leather. *She* was his first thought, because her figure seemed feminine, despite the masculine bias of "le chat". Stiff felt ears extended from the cowl that completely covered her head. Gauze cat's eyes sewn into the mask concealed her own eyes from view, and a few dark lines suggesting a muzzle and whiskers had been drawn in over the face. The thief's feet were shod with boots like thick socks with rubber soles, and she had curious metal-clawed gloves on her hands. All her clothes were a fetching azure.

The thief was nearly as tall as Janvier with a muscular build distinctive enough that he thought he'd recognize her another time by physique alone. As he studied the thief's person, he became aware of a physical attraction, the first such he'd felt for over two years, and something he'd assumed he would never feel again.

"Le Chat Azur, I presume. Or should it be la chatte?" Despite the hackneyed words, which were all he could come up with on the spur of the moment, Janvier was pleased that his voice sounded steady and strong. The thief's sudden appearance had come as a serious shock.

"I use le chat because our language is unhappy with the non-binary. La chatte determines the feminine more definitely than le chat fixes masculinity. Anyway, I often prefer a masculine mode."

Janvier bowed. "Forgive me, then. Le Chat Azur it is."

The thief bowed in turn. "Commissaire Janvier. Enchanté."

At that moment, more than anything else in the world Janvier wanted to appear cool, collected, and even suave, if it were possible. He handed them the just-opened bottle of cola, and then as he realized they'd have to pull their cowl up to drink, he turned his back so they wouldn't be revealing even that small part of their face.

"Such a gentleman! I'm impressed."

Janvier heard the motion of fabric, heard them drinking, and when he heard them replace their mask, he turned back to receive the bottle, half-empty now. To be courteous he took a sip and realized how thirsty he'd become, so he drank the rest of the bottle.

They faced each other wordlessly for a moment. Janvier felt he had nothing to do with his hands, so he clasped them behind his back and tried to stand still with a neutral expression on his face. It would have become excruciating after more than a second or two, but the thief rescued him by speaking first.

"And so discreet! No impertinent questions about how I snuck up on him, no clumsy threats to execute an arrest for breaking and entering. It's almost like he's not a detective at all!"

"I presume you wouldn't have appeared so dramatically before me if you didn't have some objective in mind apart from the theft of an obscure painting whose artist isn't even known to history. I'm willing to hear you out before making an arrest on a minor charge."

"Intelligent, too! Commissaire, please forgive the imposition. And the drama. I assure you there's good reason for the former, and I couldn't resist the latter. The fact is, I need your help."

Janvier offered a little half-bow. "The motto of the police is 'render assistance.' If I can be of service in any way consistent with the law and my duties, I am happy to help. However, I must confess—"

"You don't see how you can reasonably help a thief in the practice of their profession? You're not sure why my request should trump the usual requirements of the law, namely, to arrest thieves? You're mystified why I shouldn't have simply approached you openly, perhaps at your office at the Quai des Serpents?"

"All of those things, yes."

"If you're willing, I'll show you the nature of the problem, this very minute. Without this practical demonstration you would never believe me, and such a demonstration would be impossible at your office. In fact, it's really most convenient here ... and now. Please give me your hand."

At this point Janvier was inclined to raise objections, but having been so thoroughly complimented for his poise and complaisance he felt it would be less than suave to demur. So, knowing full well he was being manipulated, he offered his hand anyway. Le Chat Azur took it firmly, carefully avoiding contacting his skin with the sharp clawlike extensions on the fingertips of their gloves.

"Do those tiny things really help you climb?"

"Surprisingly well," they said. "Maraging steel, ground down to razor sharpness and magically strengthened. If not for your officers outside, I could have climbed the outer wall without even using a gecko spell on my gloves."

Much as he wanted to ask how they *had* gained entry, he resisted the urge. Sang-froid, not to mention savoir-faire, required a certain coolness in the circumstances.

"You'll soon see how I managed it. Come on. Hold tight."

They led him out of the gallery room and back onto the landing, where they went upstairs. Up to the seventh floor, the top gallery level. Janvier felt a curious coldness in the air, an electric prickling running up and down his spine that was almost pleasurable. The stairway seemed darker now, the gas lights on the walls providing less illumination than before. Could the baron have turned them down for the night?

"Yes," they breathed. "It's working. I thought it would, despite your resistance to sorcery. This isn't an actual spell, you see. It's something more ... primal."

It seemed they knew about his disability. Janvier had been wondering if that was the reason they had selected him rather than any other police officer with more experience. Had le Chat Azur also pulled some strings in the department to have him assigned to this case? Janvier couldn't believe a thief had such power, but otherwise the coincidence was too much for him to swallow.

Le Chat Azur walked up to the eighth floor with no attempt at stealth, like they didn't care if they woke the baron, or as if they knew he wasn't there. The gas lamps now showed no more than a faint glow. The thief led Janvier by the hand through almost complete darkness.

"Here," they murmured in his ear. "The ladder to the roof. There will be light up there. Just ... don't be too surprised by what you see, all right? I'm going to maintain body contact with you as you climb."

The thief guided Janvier's hand to a rung of the wall-mounted ladder. Before letting go of his hand, they placed their other hand up against the back of his neck, which caused those electric shivers along his spine to intensify. A frisson shuddered through him, so pleasurable a sensation he almost moaned aloud.

As he placed his foot on the first rung, le Chat Azur reached out to hold his ankle.

"Slowly," they whispered. "Don't break contact. To the top."

Maintaining contact slowed his ascent, but it was just four meters up and so it didn't take long.

"There," the thief said as he approached the top. "You may feel some resistance. Just go up to the roof. Through that dark patch."

Janvier looked up. The general gloom of the little ladder shaft to the roof was exceeded by a rectangle of absolute blackness just above his head. He reached out for it, and instead of the trapdoor he was still expecting, his hand encountered something flexible and resilient, an elastic membrane, maybe. He pushed against it and his fingers went through it. Reaching out, he found the stone lip of the roof above so he clambered upward. He felt the thief's hand on his bottom, boosting him up, perhaps; were the pricks from the blades on their glove pressing through the seat of his trousers intentional? And if so—he wrenched his thoughts back to the immediate situation.

Janvier was profoundly reluctant to touch the zone of darkness with his head, but he felt he could hardly back down now, so taking a deep breath he pressed on through.

•　　•　　•

There had been a moment of dizzy discontinuity, like Janvier had fainted and immediately regained consciousness, but that couldn't have happened or he would have fallen. It was brighter up here, the light from the sky, the stars, illuminating the roof but—he stopped short. This wasn't the same roof as before. He wasn't in Lutèce anymore. The stars overhead were unfamiliar, a vast blue nebula taking up half the sky, gorgeous and terrible.

He lowered his gaze to the city below the impossible sky ... it *was* a city, just ... not his. This tower seemed to be quite similar to the baron's Tour des Corbeaux, but in disrepair, even in ruins, with stones missing from the cornice and a slight angle to the rooftop. Instead of respectable apartment buildings, only mounds of debris surrounded the tower's little plaza. Further off, there were islands in the broken maelstrom of rubble in which buildings still stood, but this city seemed to have suffered some terrible catastrophe because most of it had been reduced to piles of shattered masonry.

There were some uncanny correspondences with the Lutèce he knew, however. Off to the north, that massive dark hill must be the Butte de Mars, though *his* butte wasn't surmounted by a shining white palace glowing strangely in the starlight. And off to the south ... yes, the black snake of the Rivière Serpentine followed the same course he knew so well.

"You see?" The thief's words came as they climbed up onto the roof behind him. "A demonstration was necessary. It would have been impossible to tell you the story in your office."

"Right," he said. "What is this place? Where have you taken me?"

"I don't know for sure. I don't know anything about this place for sure. I've only spent a small amount of time here. It frightens me a great deal. But I think this is the *real* Lutèce. The city behind the city."

"What does that even mean?"

"I don't know! I'm just saying what it *feels* like to me. You're the first I've tried to bring through with me to the other side."

"How hard can it be to discover? Why doesn't the baron know about this ... this portal in his own tower?"

"It doesn't appear unless you've been initiated into the mystery. Through some contact with someone else who has access to the phenomenon. If you'd come up here by yourself you wouldn't have found anything unusual. But I found the way, and now I've shown it to you. You'll probably be able to go through on your own from now on, but I don't think it's a good idea. Not until you've learned more about the place."

"Initiated ... how were you initiated? Who showed *you* the way?"

Le Chat Azur flinched and lost their smooth demeanor. "I ... I followed someone in. It's possible under the right circumstances. They didn't know I was following them. I—You want to know more about who it was, and how I happened to be following them. I mean to tell you, too, but it's—it's not easy. After we get home again, all right?"

"As you wish. But that one aside, you must have anticipated I want to ask a million other questions."

"Most of which I can't answer. And some that I can you still probably wouldn't believe the answers to. Let's just take a walk outside, shall we? You'll get a feel for the city. that way."

Janvier was silent for a moment. "Very well," he said at last, knowing he couldn't coerce information out of the thief, so he really was at their mercy as regards any further explanation.

"Good. But before we descend, I want to direct your attention to a few points of interest."

Janvier wasn't surprised when they pointed to the palatial white structure atop the Butte de Mars.

"That place is strange. It's dangerous at night, too. Which means you'd have to spend a full day here if you wanted to explore it, because you can only come and go for an hour or so after midnight. I don't want to strand you here, so I'll take you to the nearest return point before the window closes."

"Why is it dangerous?"

"The ... inhabitants of this city seem to like visiting it during the nighttime hours. We ought to be safe enough on the ruined streets down below, however, moving between here and the equivalent of the Place des Lutins in this city. That's our return point. But I also want you to take note of another destination. Look over there, out where the 8th arrondissement would be in Lutèce."

Janvier looked. The area was unlit, but from what he could make out the buildings there appeared to be intact. In Lutèce, the 8th combined a fancy shopping district with some government buildings as well as one of the most exclusive residential neighborhoods in the city, inhabited mainly by old noble families. Even though he couldn't see the buildings clearly, the difference between that district and others that had been reduced to rubble was clear.

"It's dark. I can't make out any details."

"Yes. But focus on it. Try to project your gaze. That has an effect here."

Janvier didn't know what they were asking. But he stared at the area of darkened buildings nevertheless, and after a moment he saw it, a strange sparkling aura around the neighborhood, like the halo he'd seen around a laboratory demonstration of a sodium vapor lamp when he was at university.

"What *is* that place?"

"I ... I can't say. But it's something to look into."

Janvier was going to ask what street in Lutèce might correspond with the one this building was on, but le Chat Azur raised their hand.

"Later, all right? Let's go downstairs now. I want to escort you back to our city before anything gets in our way."

Janvier glanced at the ladder shaft. The peculiar zone of absolute blackness he'd had to push through on the way up was gone.

"What happened—"

"We used it up. On its own it lasts for an hour or so, but it vanishes when you pass through it. The portal will regenerate at midnight tomorrow. That's why we have to go to the Place des Lutins. It's got the nearest other passage back to our world that I know of."

"I see."

"I'll go first with a light spell," the thief said.

Janvier reminded them, "Don't get too close to me or it'll go out."

"Ugh. Must make life difficult at times."

"You have no idea."

Le Chat Azur descended the ladder, and down below he saw the bloom of their magelight. When Janvier climbed down, by the light shining from the thief's palm he could see the tower interior was in sad shape here compared to the one in Lutèce, with cracks in the cyclopean stonework and even some stones missing from the wall.

"There's one more thing I want to show you while we're here," le Chat Azur said. "It's horrible, but fascinating too. Completely safe, however."

They led him into the central room for the top floor and shined their light around until it picked out one particular doorway.

"That's the same room as the baron's chamber. Follow me."

Janvier gave the thief a few strides to avoid interfering with their spell and entered the room. An old four-poster bed made out of corroded black iron was the only piece of furniture, its bedclothes long since decayed and even the mattress mostly gone, just a few bits of old fabric remaining over a matrix of rusty springs. And on it lay a dead body.

Whoever it was had died long ago in a supine position, and their body was now little more than a skeleton with a few bits of leathery skin still attached here and there. Le Chat Azur directed their light at the corpse and Janvier flinched when the skull came more clearly into view. It was exactly the same as the skull he had hallucinated earlier, appearing from beneath the living baron's melting skin. Exactly the same, the same shade of pale yellowy-brown bone, the same pattern of missing teeth, the same gaping orbits ... there could be no mistake.

For Janvier the horror was more philosophical than visceral; he wasn't usually repulsed so much as saddened by the sight of death itself. Though he'd only had one murder case to deal with, he'd occasionally had to handle accidental or old-age deaths as an arrondissement officer. Only the murder case had traumatized him, because of the wanton malice and monstrous cruelty of the criminal.

Seeing the skull beneath the baron's face that morning had been horrible for Janvier largely because it was impossible, but seeing an actual skull wasn't a problem in itself. It was the similarity or perhaps the identity of the skull in his vision with the one right here that set him back on his heels. The resonance of vision and memory exceeded his rational comprehension.

"Look closely," the thief said, which seemed like an act of cruelty on their part, but they couldn't know how he'd been affected.

Le Chat Azur walked nearer to the bed, their magelight illuminating the body more brightly. Janvier followed their pointing hand with his gaze and saw what they were indicating: long slender bones beneath the skeletal corpse, connected to its upper back. Wings.

The fascination Janvier felt as a result of this revelation banished his unease. He approached more closely and the thief backed away to avoid interference with their spell. Janvier picked at something stuck in a coil of a spring under where the corpse's shoulder bones reposed and extracted it, the spring giving off a rusty screech as it flexed in his grip. He'd pulled out a stiff curving quill with a few fluffy black barbs still attached.

"Baron Corbeau, indeed," Janvier said. "Or perhaps, le corbeau baron."

"I know, right?" the thief said. "I thought this would be a good way to show you. I've found a few other ancient corpses in other buildings. All had wings."

Janvier looked down at the floor around the bed. Yes. More black feathers, some of them no more than little downy curls, others longer and more fully intact, perhaps primaries for the wings.

Janvier had a lot to think about, and le Chat Azur had nothing more to show him in the tower, so they descended in mutual silence. They led him down much the same angled sequence of flights that they'd ascended in Lutèce's version of the tower till they got to the first story, then down the sweeping grand stairs to the ground floor. The foyer here was faintly illuminated by the eerie blue radiance of the vast nebula shining through a shattered doorway.

The thief extinguished their light spell and they walked out into the night of this strange city. As he stood for a moment on the ruined street taking in the scene, Janvier felt an overwhelming sense of desolation and loss. This wasn't his city and the inhabitants weren't his people, but they'd lost something grand and beautiful all the same.

"Are you all right?" Le Chat Azur put their hand on his shoulder, and at their touch the feeling faded, replaced by something like normalcy, or even strength. Janvier realized with some surprise he was taking pleasure in the contact.

"I'm fine."

"Good. I'm sorry. I should have known this wouldn't be easy. I had a bad time my first night here, and it got worse when I realized I couldn't go back the way I came. I had to hide out all day, hoping not to be found, hoping I'd find a way back the next night."

They made their way through ruined streets for a time, sometimes having to pick their way over rubble where some building had collapsed into the street.

•　　　•　　　•

This world's Place des Lutins would have been similar to Lutèce's if it weren't mostly in ruins. It looked like this too might once have been an entertainment district, as Janvier could identify a mound of rubble as a fallen marquee that might have fronted a theater or a club and there, in a protected corner of still-standing masonry, a recognizable outdoor cafe table.

Janvier noticed a depression in the street that was now full of debris and earth but must once have offered access to an underground level as he could just make out the top of a stairway. An ornate metal framework stood in front of the depression like a symbolic archway, and from it a sign depended with the word "Metropolitain" still legible in stylized enamel, green on a white background.

"Do you know what this means?" he asked.

Le Chat Azur shook their head. "No idea."

"The people who lived here. They may have had wings, but they spoke our language. And if this place is as old as it seems ... Perhaps they weren't affected by the Palimpsest Event. In our world, a sign more than 532 years old would have been erased. There could be surviving records here somewhere. A library, maybe."

"Maybe," they said. "I haven't found one. There's an old street sign nearby if it interests you. It says 'Place Pigalle' rather than 'Place des Lutins'. Of course there's no Pigalle in our Lutèce, it's just what it must have been called here. But let's hurry now. If we don't get to the passage in time it might close for the night before you can pass through it."

The thief led Janvier over a difficult field of jagged rubble to a mostly intact wall. There it was, a mysterious patch of absolute blackness filling a broken gap in the wall like a spiderweb.

"You first," they said.

"Wait. Where does this go?"

"A music shop on the Place des Lutins. They'll be closed for the night."

Janvier was still full of questions he wanted to ask. But it would be more convenient to discuss this strange new world back home with no time pressure, so he approached the wall. Just like with the tower, a mysterious aura of darkness surrounded him as he neared the portal, and again he felt that strange resistance before his extended hand pushed through. He emerged as promised in the interior of a shop, illuminated faintly here in the back by light from the street filtering through the plate glass storefront. Guitars, violins, and accordions hung on the far wall, and on a little platform in front of him a double bass was set up as if ready to be played on a club's stage. He turned to see a blank wall. That uncanny darkness was already fading. Le Chat Azur did not emerge, and a moment later the phenomenon was gone, vanished completely.

4

TOO LATE, JANVIER REALIZED he'd been maneuvered through the portal and le Chat Azur had no intention of following. He shook his head. Maybe he didn't understand what was going on, but there was nothing he could do about it now.

He stumbled through the darkened shop, nearly tripping over a drum set before making his way to the better illuminated area near the front door. From there he exited onto the public square. Several clubs and bistros remained open at this hour and a reassuring number of completely ordinary, nonavian pedestrians were on the street.

Trying not to think too much about what he'd just experienced, Janvier returned on foot to the Tour des Corbeaux, which was only a few minutes away through Lutèce's well-lit streets. The police officer currently on duty at the door was astonished at his appearance. It was just past 1:00 AM; Janvier still had five hours of guard duty left to serve.

"Commissaire!" the officer exclaimed, saluting. "Did you go out during my partner's shift? He didn't tell me."

Janvier forced a chuckle. "Not to worry. I assume nothing has happened in my absence?"

"No, sir. All quiet."

"Excellent."

Janvier entered the tower, not without some creepy apprehension. He walked up through the floors; all seemed normal. He spent some time thinking about the whole situation. Le Chat Azur may have been telling him the truth about the short window of time during which access to the other world was possible, but they'd also gone to some trouble to limit their conversation, including cutting the connection between them and leaving him in this world to wonder. Surely, they must realize the questions and considerations that would pass through his head. On the other hand, they hadn't even tried to extract a promise from him not to tell anyone. If he really had been *initiated*, he might be able to conduct others between worlds the way they had conducted him. Was it his duty to report the whole incident? Was he honor-bound to say nothing and protect what was at least an implied confidence?

The night ended … eventually. Janvier counted himself lucky to be more or less awake and attentive at 5:00 AM when Baron Corbeau surprised him by descending from his rooms to the gallery. It was still dark, but the city's birds had just begun chirping.

"Good morning, Commissaire," the baron said. "I trust the night was … uneventful?"

"Yes." Even though the night *had* been uneventful the way Baron Corbeau meant, even though it was at worst a very minor lie, Janvier hesitated for a moment before answering; he hated any kind of fabrication or deception.

Janvier added, "I imagine you'll want to tour your collection, just to be sure?"

"I hadn't … contemplated doing so. But … since you suggest it …"

It took Baron Corbeau the better part of an excruciating hour to verify nothing had been taken. All the while, Janvier wondered how the baron would react to the news that a portal to another world was located in his tower. Would he raise a cynical eyebrow? Show outrage at such a ridiculous idea? Or ... perhaps ... would he acknowledge it as a known fact? Le Chat Azur wasn't the only one in on the secret. Someone had initiated them. Yet another mystery Janvier needed to solve.

Baron Corbeau had just finished his verification tour when Frémont showed up at five minutes to six, the young inspector a little bleary-eyed due to what must have been a late night, but cheerful enough in a fetching spring outfit: a jonquil suit with a rose necktie over a white shirt, a pink carnation as a boutonniere, and shoes that matched the tie.

The baron returned to his work upstairs, whatever it was he was doing, and now Janvier faced a dilemma: let Frémont in on the secret or not? Not here and now, he decided. He hated leaving Frémont in the dark even for a short while, but it would be too difficult to tell him now, with no way to prove the truth of his words.

•   •   •

Janvier returned home with the intention of sleeping until noon. He fell asleep easily but when he woke up it was only nine and he felt not a bit tired. He sighed, got dressed, and strolled to his usual breakfast cafe, Les Tasses d'Antan, the morning newspaper folded under his arm. He sat down at an outside table; Janvier enjoyed people-watching, and it was always pleasant to exchange greetings with his neighbors as they went about their errands. His café au lait and pain au chocolat consumed, Janvier realized he'd neglected to check in with headquarters.

Janvier launched out of his chair and made ten meters before he had to turn back to leave payment for his breakfast. Then he ran to his flat to place the call. He was asked to hold. After some delay, Inspecteur-general Lambert came on the line.

"Ah, Janvier," he said. "So good of you to check in."

As was often the case, Janvier wasn't sure whether Lambert was being sarcastic or not.

"We're having a meeting to discuss le Chat Azur at ten. Can you be there?"

"Of course, Monsieur."

Janvier thought this was more than strange; he'd just been assigned the case and no crime had ostensibly been committed. What could the matter be?

•　　　•　　　•

Janvier made it to Lambert's staff room just in time; the meeting was about to begin and the usual civilities had already been exchanged. But this wasn't Lambert's regular staff meeting. Two unusual guests were present, one whom Janvier had never met before in person but only recognized from her address to his graduating class at the university. Comtesse du Bois d'Acaire was the directeur-general of the Police Nationale, the umbrella organization into which the Police Judiciaire fit. She was accompanied by another figure only occasionally seen at the Quai des Serpents, Lambert's boss Préfet de Police Pierre Moreau. Both these notables' offices were at the ministry of the interior's main building in the 8th arrondissement.

The elegantly turned-out comtesse, in a smart navy-blue pantsuit over a white blouse, was known as a bold, decisive administrator. She was also a member of the national assembly for the conservative blue party. Her appointment was political as she had no prior experience on the force; she reported directly to the minister of the interior, and her main job was to liaise between the government and the police. Moreau, in contrast, a balding middle-aged man wearing an ill-fitting blue suit with red pinstripes, was a career civil servant who had served through half a dozen changes of government, shedding controversies like water off a duck's plumage.

Apart from the white-haired Inspecteur-General Lambert whose meeting it was, at this hour in a dove-gray morning coat, Commissaire Renard of Art Crimes was also in attendance, a middle-aged man with shining black hair and a pencil-thin mustache. To Janvier he resembled a suave, elegant river otter. Renard wore a rich brown wool suit with a gold tie.

For a change, the usually self-assured Lambert appeared to be uncomfortable in his own staff room, no doubt due to the presence of his two superiors.

"Janvier," he said curtly. "Good of you to make it on short notice. At the ministry's request, perhaps you can give us a brief report of your doings over the last twenty-four hours?"

Janvier had been rather concerned about what role he might be asked to play in this meeting, but he could manage a simple report. Lying by omission pained him nearly as much as outright fabrication, but he withheld his strange encounter with the thief and also the mysterious ruined city. The one point he added that he might have held back was that he had received his own calling-card at home in addition to the one delivered to Baron Corbeau.

"Curious," the comtesse said, her first words of the meeting.

"I wonder whether a crime is really going to take place here," Janvier said. He noticed Commissaire Renard giving him a glance, and was that the slightest negative head-shake?

But the comtesse didn't seem annoyed. She ignored the remark and moved on.

"Needless to say, wanton criminality is an embarrassment to the ministry, and to the police as well."

Lambert opened his mouth, but the comtesse raised her hand. "I'm sure you're doing your best, Inspecteur-general, but you will correct me if I'm wrong that there are no leads, are there? No entrée within the League of Thieves to exploit, and no clue to the thief's identity beyond their nom du crime. That's what I shall tell the minister, and that's no doubt what he will tell the press."

Janvier blinked but said nothing. He would have thought the police brass and the ministry would both want to at least give the appearance of activity rather than admitting to an immediate failure. And what kind of failure could it be when no crime had been committed so far as the police brass knew?

Lambert closed his mouth. He shook his head. "No, Comtesse. You are correct."

The meeting went on for a while. Janvier had the feeling that he didn't understand the language they were speaking. Nothing quite made sense to him. No further business seemed to be done, and yet another 45 minutes of back and forth elapsed before they concluded, mainly remarks by the directeur-general and the préfet, both of whom would have been able to converse more easily at their own offices. Fortunately, he wasn't called to say anything further. As they filed out of the room, Renard tapped Janvier on the shoulder.

"A moment of your time?"

"Of course, Commissaire," Janvier said.

"I'm sure this meeting must have confused you. Perhaps you'd like to hear my thoughts about what was going on in there?"

"I'd be very grateful."

Renard took Janvier downstairs and across the street to the Brasserie de la Vipère, a popular dining spot for police officers, lawyers, and magistrates from the criminal court.

They sat down in a secluded corner, if not a quiet one. The Art Crimes squad leader made a show of contemplating the menu. At length he ordered the langoustine; Janvier chose the choucroute garnie. Renard hardly said a word till he was finished eating, and Janvier had no choice but to remain silent till the plates were cleared away. When at last the table was clear, he leaned forward.

"My brother is a secretary," Renard said.

"Oh, really?"

"Yes. He works for M. Alfonse, the shadow finance minister. And so I hear quite a bit of political gossip. Of course, you know what I mean when I say the shadow finance minister."

"Of course. The opposition front-bencher who has the finance portfolio, the one who will most likely become finance minister himself if the reds win the next general election."

Renard put both hands on the table in front of him. He lowered his voice.

"I suppose you also know what I mean if I just say 'shadow minister' with no other modifier?"

Janvier hesitated. "There's this … what would you call it? An urban legend? A sort of political bogeyman?"

"Go on."

"I've heard it forever, or rather overheard bits of it. The kind of thing people talk about at the bar. The story goes he's the power behind every government, red or blue, and has been since the Palimpsest Event. Of course that would make him superhuman. He supposedly doesn't care much about most government business, but on the rare occasion someone in government does something he doesn't like, proposes some legislation he's opposed to, for example—Then he takes action."

"And that action would be?"

"Something drastic, peremptory, and usually totally inexplicable. Like making the legislator change their views overnight. Or sometimes making them disappear completely. But this is just—"

"Just the reality the leaders of the government in both parties don't like to admit to. Because if they do, guess what will happen to them?"

"You can't be serious!"

"But I am. And no, I'm not particularly thankful to my brother for enlightening me on this score, because I would have been perfectly happy living in blissful ignorance. Sometimes when I get involved in something political and high level, like today's meeting, I can smell the shadow minister's influence. Today the chief of police decided to admit public defeat without even making an attempt to catch the thief. That may not be due to the shadow minister directly, but if it's not I expect it's due to someone high up perceiving, or at least thinking they perceive, the shadow minister's intentions. If they change their minds again, it will be because they realized they guessed wrong."

"Well," Janvier said, uncomfortable with these conspiratorial confidences, "thanks for the warning."

"I didn't mean it just as a vague, general warning," Renard said. "I wouldn't have exposed myself like that, just to make you unhappy with ominous talk about something that can't be proven. But the thing is, this business with le Chat Azur … I didn't request your assistance with the baron's complaint. That came from above, probably from higher than Lambert, either the comtesse or the minister of the interior, but Lambert told me you were going to be assigned to it, and he told me to pretend it was my idea. We're always busy in Art Crimes, but we can stretch ourselves when we have to. And it's a shit assignment, too, for a theft that wasn't going to happen because Baron Corbeau has nothing worth stealing in the first place. So that's evidence of something strange going on."

Renard grimaced. "And now, today and this irrational meeting we just had … I don't pretend to know exactly what's going on, Janvier, but I'm just saying, watch yourself on this one. Don't speak up, don't get clever ideas. Like when you doubted a crime was going to take place? You probably did no harm, but it's best not to be too original. Just do what you're told on this case, is my advice. And if you see that kind of thing in future, weird behavior from the brass, don't complain too loudly."

5

A S JANVIER GOT UP FROM LUNCH, he felt the fatigue of his late night of adventure and watchkeeping settling heavily on his shoulders. More than that, he was profoundly unhappy with Renard for subjecting him to this unwelcome confidence. Over a single day, Janvier had the metaphysical foundation of his world swept out from under his feet, and worse, he'd been told that the admittedly stodgy but generally liberal democracy in which he lived was secretly subject to a whimsical autocrat's arbitrary decrees. It was really too much, he felt, for him to handle on his own.

Janvier's first course of action was to stop by the squad room, but de l'Épée wasn't present, probably en route to the baron's, and of course Frémont was still on duty at the tower. He left notes for them in their mailboxes, asking them to call him either at the office or at home as soon as they could so they could discuss what he could only call "the situation", not wanting to give any hint of what he really meant to talk about.

•   •   •

Bothering a couple of Renard's people over at Art Crimes, Janvier discovered that some pre-Palimpsest furnishings and objets d'art were indeed valuable, but due to lack of attestable provenance of designer or workshop never achieved the heights of modern masterpieces with verifiable histories. Liqueur and spirits from that era were completely unknown and would undoubtedly fetch a high price at auction if any were put up for sale.

The specialist he talked to, Inspecteur Delacroix, told him, "It's an intriguing idea. But I think not something a top League thief would go after. Not now, anyway. Because the bottles would be nameless and obscure, you see? No notoriety, no celebrity associated with the theft itself, and no special security guarding the wine cellar, either. If the thief were hard up for cash, just maybe they'd steal the bottles en passant as low-hanging fruit, but such a theft wouldn't score any points with the League."

Janvier's other bit of research involved looking at the police neighborhood map of the 8th arrondissement, specifically the wealthy neighborhood to which le Chat Azur had directed his attention. It was difficult to relate the map to his distant view of the corresponding district in the ruined city. He thumbed through the address book listings, hoping for some particular name to leap out at him, but though he recognized a number of prominent old noble families, many of whom were in the conservative government, he had no reason to choose one over another as being of special interest.

•   •   •

By the time Janvier got home at 3:00 PM, he'd come to a decision. Picking up the phone, he rang up the university switchboard, and when they answered, he asked for ÉCarlate 12.

"Alexandra Janvier. De l'Ordre Écarlate. Fire and light, our specialty." She was always flippant on the phone.

"Mother? It's me."

"Ah! Jules! So good of you to remember your mother!"

He was about to pour out the reasons for his call, but then it occurred to him how easy it was for anyone at either the phone company or the university switchboard to listen in. And he felt a little wave of disgust for even having that thought. That kind of worry wasn't something he'd ever signed up for.

"Mother," he said, "do you happen to be free for dinner tonight?"

"As it happens, I am. But why so formal?"

"It's just we haven't spoken in quite a long time, and I thought I should make amends properly with a nice dinner."

They'd dined together just three days ago. But he wanted to come up with a plausible excuse for a meeting in case anyone was listening.

"But Jules—" Something in his tone of voice must have warned her. Perhaps she thought it was a gag of some kind, perhaps she thought it was more serious, but she didn't complain about the facts. "That's very sweet of you. Where should we meet?"

"How about La Tram Bleu? Say, seven?"

"That sounds lovely, dear. I'll see you then."

He made the reservation by phone and then Janvier tried to nap for the rest of the afternoon. When he awoke he checked in at headquarters to make sure he hadn't missed any new developments. Nothing had been stolen, anyway. Frémont had left him a message saying he would stop by the Tour des Corbeaux at 10:00 PM that night, so both he and de l'Épée would be present for whatever Janvier chose to tell them.

•   •   •

La Tram Bleu was a fancy restaurant in the 12th arrondissement, the interior made up to look like a streetcar, if a tram ever had blue-velvet-upholstered seats, shimmering lapis-inset wall panels, and tropical wood dining tables. The wait staff wore Transit Lutèce uniforms but the bill of fare ran around ten times as much as a traveler's dinner at the Gare Central Café.

•　　　•　　　•

As a junior inspector with the Patrouille Communautaire, Janvier had been paid a modest salary, equivalent to a store clerk or an apprentice artisan. His pay had risen enormously as a commissaire in the Police Judiciaire, but he hadn't indulged himself in a lavish lifestyle and so the price of the check at La Tram Blue was an unusual expense for him. This parsimonious behavior is no doubt laudable, but for me it was really incomprehensible.

•　　　•　　　•

Janvier looked up from his menu as his mother entered the restaurant. The professeur was as dashing as ever in her red professorial cape. She'd confessed once that a serious motivation for her doctorate was not having to worry about what to wear thereafter, as the working attire of a Scarlet Order researcher and lecturer combined the formal and the flamboyant and was as appropriate in the laboratory or the classroom as at the restaurant or the theater.

Janvier had slipped the maitresse d' a few bills to find them a secluded table, so there was no one close by to overhear their conversation. His mother seated herself and smiled at him.

"What's going on, Jules? Why the foolery on the telephone?" Alexandra Janvier was never one for beating around the bush.

"I—let's order and get our food. I don't want to have to look over my shoulder for the waiter."

"I see. It's that bad, is it? Very well."

This was after all one of the most fashionable restaurants in the city, so Janvier tried to devote some attention to the menu. He found himself thinking that if he skipped the starter and the salad and the soup, the meal would go faster, so perversely he ordered oeufs farcis with caviar, potage parmentier, salade niçoise, and a sauteed breast of chicken in a cream sauce with capers and shallots. And though he would have said he wouldn't taste a bite, his contrary nature wound up distracting him with the savory flavors of the meal, and so his belly was quite full by the time he got around to the point of the dinner.

"Which secret should I start with first?" Janvier asked. "The mysterious ruined city accessible from Lutèce via magical portals?" He trailed off, wondering if there was any way she could possibly believe what he was telling her.

But his mother appeared to be taking him seriously. "There's something more important than that?"

"Yes. I was just told today that the shadow minister is real. In earnest, by someone I trust. A mastermind who controls the government."

His mother sat back. "I suppose I'm supposed to raise an eyebrow and ask if this is some sort of joke. But I know you too well for that, Jules. You wouldn't try this on me if you didn't believe it."

"Mom ..."

She patted his hand. "So tell me the story. I'm listening."

He recounted the story of the last two days, leaving nothing out. It was a great relief to be able to reveal every detail; he hadn't realized how stressed he'd been by the need to hold it back. When he was done, his mother leaned forward in her chair, an eager gleam in her eyes.

"Do you believe all that?" Janvier asked. "I'm not sure I would if I was hearing it from someone else."

"I do. Much as I want to see this strange place with my own eyes. I've always suspected *something*, you see. You know I work with high-energy sorcery. From time to time I've seen anomalies in my experimental results. Hints of phenomena that appear to originate from outside what I might rather poetically call the walls of the world. And when I've tried to explore these anomalies with experiments tailored for the purpose, I've had promising lines of research terminated without sensible explanations from the College of Magic review committee. So I've noticed, let us say, a hostile influence at times. It never occurred to me to concentrate this influence in the person of the shadow minister, however. I just assumed I'd rubbed a department chair the wrong way or something like that."

Janvier said, "I hate the idea of this invisible influence permeating everything. It's not such a great secret either if I could learn it from Renard so easily. And yet this shadow minister, whether it's a person or some kind of agency or conspiracy, has never been publicly exposed. Frankly it makes me sick to think about it."

"My poor Jules! This must have been terribly distressing."

"It was ... disturbing. Either or both these things would have been bad enough on their own. Coming together, it's really been a shock. But listen, mother, I don't want you to get into trouble, either."

"Jules! I am not a complete ninny. I wouldn't betray your confidence. Although ..."

"What?"

"I do have some colleagues whose judgment I trust, both in the Scarlet Order and elsewhere around the university. Without telling them anything explicit ... I could sound them out. See if they've been sensing the same things I did about strange influences coming down from above. That kind of thing. And of course, the university library is the best in the city. We have an enormous esoterica collection no one ever bothers with because it's all myths and fantasy. I could look for references to your city there."

"I trust your judgment, mother. It's just ... you know how horrified I would be if I'd made trouble for you. The stories I've heard about the shadow minister are not very nice ones."

"I promise I'll be discreet."

Janvier sighed. He knew that of all the people he could have told, his mother was the safest and most responsible. He also knew that it was totally unreasonable to expect her to sit on her hands and do nothing with the information. He hadn't even been sure she'd believe him, had concocted fantasy scenarios where she'd try to get him into care to deal with delusions—

"So tell me more about le Chat Azur," his mother said suddenly. "They sound interesting."

"I didn't have the chance to say very much to them. I think that was by design. They had some objective in mind they didn't share with me."

"Jules. A glamorous, mysterious thief leads you literally by the hand into another world, then ditches you back here for unknown reasons. You must have had *some* thoughts about them."

"I don't see that I *must* have," Janvier said. "But in fact I admit that I *did*. I mean, they were wearing a slinky catsuit with functioning claws. And they were masked. Extremely mysterious, and alluring, too. But I think even my totally shameless concierge wouldn't have hit on them in the circumstances, if that's what you were hoping I'd do."

"That's fine," his mother said. "I was just wondering what you thought of them, is all. Because it seems that they sought you out ..."

•   •   •

Janvier had gone through the usual eager and chaotic series of experimental liaisons in high school as soon as sex became legal for him, but his relationships had tailed off at the university and since the episode with the Butcher of Mars he'd been chaste for the last two years. He'd told himself he needed time to recover before dating again or contracting with courtesans, and then he'd told himself he just wasn't interested in romance anymore, or sex either. Much as I like to see people enjoying themselves and finding conjugal bliss too for that matter, it's not my place to pry. Of course, some people are asexual and aromantic, and good for them. However, rightly, or wrongly, his mother thought it was *her place to offer some gentle prodding, and perhaps she was right, too, because she put some thoughts in Janvier's head that he might not have had otherwise.*

• • •

"And speaking of caution and prudence," she added, "I do hope you don't intend to perform any independent investigation of this strange new world. Le Chat Azur may not have been entirely honest with you, but it does sound like it might be a very dangerous place to explore with no guidance from someone familiar with the place. Without some powerful magical support, it might be very risky indeed."

"Mother, are you suggesting—"

"Me? Oh! You think just because I happen to be a tenured professeur of the Scarlet Order who specializes in powerful spells of energy manipulation, three-time winner of the Prix Phénix in the all-Lutèce magical manifestations competition, and not least of all the one person in the world you've trusted with this secret so far, that I might be qualified to accompany you on some ill-advised intrusion into an alien world? Well, dear, I'm at your service."

Janvier could hardly say he couldn't have expected this, but he was taken aback nonetheless. "I'll take your offer under advisement," he said at last. "The thing is ... I feel terrible about concealing anything, much less something so, so earthshaking. This should be something everyone knows about, that all Lutèce can decide what to do with. I should report it to my boss, it should be in the news, the assembly should be debating it—"

"I quite agree, Jules," his mother said. "That's what *should* happen. But you seem to have accepted along with your colleague M. Renault that there's something fishy going on with your bosses and with the government. If there really is a shadow minister who meddles in public affairs whenever they see fit, then they will certainly want to control or suppress this revelation.

We'll want to manage this in a way that will give them no opportunity for intervention. And we'll want to know more about the facts of the situation before committing ourselves. Suppose the shadow minister already knows all about this world? Suppose they've been suppressing knowledge of its existence all along? And suppose they had good reason, too?"

"I wish none of this had happened," Janvier said. "For that matter, I wish there'd never been a Butcher of Mars, either. I'd like my world better that way."

His mother put her hand over his. "Oh, Jules ..." She looked up. "Are you going to tell your people? That de l'Épée has a good head on her shoulders. I like her quite a bit. And M. Frémont has a good heart, too, even if he *is* rather hopelessly yearning for you."

"Mother!"

"What, you hadn't noticed? I should have thought it was obvious."

·   ·   ·

In fact Janvier had noticed Frémont's occasional subtle suggestion, and if they had been peers and if he had still been romantically active, he might even have followed up. But given that he was Richard's superior it was easier to pretend total ignorance. More good judgment of the sort that I personally abhor.

·   ·   ·

"I hadn't decided yet about telling them, but since you bring up the point, I believe I will. I'll soon have the opportunity to try out this initiation I may or may not have received, and if they too can see the portal, then I'll tell them. I think they can both keep the secret if I ask."

6

10:00 PM AT THE TOUR DES CORBEAUX. Nothing had happened there over the course of the day, and le Chat Azur hadn't made the news anywhere else, either, which meant the minister of the interior hadn't addressed the press yet. Frémont was true to his appointed hour, and Janvier took him and de l'Épée up to the mezzanine level of the first floor to talk because from there it appeared impossible for Baron Corbeau to casually wander downstairs and overhear them before they noticed him coming.

"I suppose you're wondering what this is all about," Janvier said.

Frémont looked at him hungrily as if he was about to bestow some earth-shattering revelation, and Janvier had to smile at the thought that in fact he was. De l'Épée merely looked attentive.

"I realize this is going to sound melodramatic," Janvier said. "But if either of you are the slightest bit uncomfortable about being let in on a confidence that has little to do with your official duty, a confidence that might even lead to, well, a certain degree of illegality, not to mention impropriety, please—"

Frémont spoke up at once. "Chief! You know we're with you. A hundred percent and all the way. We—Oh! I interrupted! I'm sorry!"

De l'Épée took the chance to speak up.

"I may not be as … emotionally demonstrative as Richard," she said, "but working with you has made something very clear to us, Commissaire. There's no question about your integrity or your commitment to the highest principles of the force. We'll support you, just as Richard says, a hundred percent."

"I'm honored," Janvier said humbly. "I want to give you as much explanation and demonstration as I can. So, if you'll be so kind as to wait with me for another two hours, I hope to be able to show you something truly unusual come midnight."

De l'Épée granted him a raised eyebrow, but it came with a smile, and Frémont was plainly having to bite his tongue to avoid asking the obvious questions.

The time till midnight passed slowly at first, but Janvier managed to get Frémont talking about his favorite nightspots (the Folies Féeriques near the Place des Lutins ranked highly). From there they moved onto cuisine, Janvier favoring Esperian pasta and sauces, de l'Épée sticking with traditional country cooking, and Frémont enthusiastic about the nuances of urban bistrot fare.

The final topic before the midnight hour rolled by was courtesans, favorite individual artistes and types. *(This was the happily and monogamously married de l'Épée's idea, incidentally; Janvier would never have brought it up himself, and Frémont wouldn't have dared.)* But since the topic had after all been broached, the younger inspector proved to be quite the aficionado. He danced around her questions regarding his particular tastes for a while before de l'Épée pinned him down, and the reason for his evasion turned out to be that many of his favorites were men who rather resembled Janvier himself in their superficial qualities.

"Fascinating," de l'Épée said with an uncharacteristically wicked gleam in her eye. "Such consistency of taste really argues for a laudably clear understanding of one's own desires."

She glanced ostentatiously at Janvier as if only then realizing his resemblance to the courtesans they'd been discussing. "But you know, come to think of it ..."

"Oh," Frémont said, desperate to distract from her point, "but of course like everyone else, the one I'm *really* dreaming of is the ondine Kefildur. Can you imagine how it must be with an elemental[3]? They can change their bodies, change sex at will! I'd happily go into debt for just an hour of their time."

Both Janvier and Frémont were relieved when de l'Épée brought out her pocket watch. "Well, enough fun and games. Your midnight hour approaches, Commissaire. Can we have the demonstration here or do we need to go somewhere for it?"

•　　•　　•

Janvier's watch chimed the hour. He'd been wondering if le Chat Azur would pull off another marvelous manifestation—he wasn't sure what balance of alien portals, thiefly skill, and conventional sorcery contributed to their appearance last time—but it seemed they had other business tonight.

"Let's go," he said. "Up the stairs to the trap door to the roof. Quietly, though; let's not disturb the baron."

---

[3] Elementals, magical entities associated with air and water, generally lived far away from Lutèce, in the wilds where humans rarely ventured. As a group these sweet-natured beings were disinclined to enter human society, not being fond of crowds, civilization, or the effort of maintaining persistent physical forms. From time to time, however, one of these curious and charming people would assume a vaguely human body and visit an outlying town or even journey to Lutèce, usually as a tourist but more rarely to dwell among humans indefinitely. The water elemental Kefildur became a citizen of the city deliberately to taste the life and pleasures of a professional courtesan and had put in the extraordinary effort necessary to develop a realistic human body as opposed to the mere blob of water more common to their people. Kefildur's exotic nature would have made them a cynosure in any event, but after an extended apprenticeship they had legitimately become one of the most skilled and enthusiastic members of the Guilde du Plaisir.

Moving from the seventh to the eighth floor, Janvier noticed no trace of the curious obscuring darkness he'd observed the night before, and so he paused at the landing, wondering whether the demonstration was going to be a failure. Then he remembered the experience of projecting his gaze toward that distant house, and how his vision had changed. He tried to recall the feeling he'd had then, the strange darkness, the curious chills down his spine ...

"Chief? What's happening?" Frémont was alarmed. "You look all ... shadowy, all of a sudden."

Janvier looked around. It was definitely darker, now.

"Take my hands," he said. "Come along with me. I can't explain all this, but I think it's not dangerous. Not yet, anyway."

De l'Épée took his left hand, and Frémont his right. It was a bit awkward as the stairs weren't wide enough for them to walk three abreast, so Frémont walked a bit to his rear, and de l'Épée rather hesitantly took the lead. They proceeded up to the eighth floor, and the obscuring effect intensified, just as it had done the previous night.

"Now," he said. "See up there? At the top of the ladder. Where the trap door should be."

"What *is* that?" de l'Épée whispered. It was the same as last night, a square of absolute darkness.

"Proof," Janvier said. "Proof of something strange. I can explain what it is, but if you're game we can pass through it and then you'll know for sure. This part was safe enough for me last night. For me and le Chat Azur, I should say."

"Le Chat Azur!" Frémont looked excited. "I knew it!"

"I can't guarantee it will be safe tonight. And I don't want to press you, either. It's just—"

De l'Épée was emphatic. "It's just you've misjudged us if you think we're going to be put off now."

"Absolutely. No way am I backing out," Frémont said.

"Very well," Janvier said. "This is going to be awkward. I think we have to maintain our bodily contact as we go up the ladder. De l'Épée, you go first. Frémont, you follow, copying me. We'll go slowly so as to make no mistake."

It really was awkward, and embarrassing too. With Janvier's grip on de l'Épée's ankle, her bottom was just above his head, and he was conscious of Frémont's similar position just below. But it was only four meters.

"All right. De l'Épée, push through the black square. There will be some resistance, but you'll feel the ledge of the roof where it should be, so just scramble up through it. I'll follow you, and Frémont, you come up after me directly, keeping your hand on me as I climb up as long as possible and not delaying at all."

"Understood," and "Yes, Chief," came from above and below. From Janvier's position it was easy enough to keep his hand on de l'Épée's ankle as she climbed the final rungs, no need to put a hand on her bottom as le Chat Azur had done for him that time they'd pricked him with her claws. Which meant—He wrenched his thoughts back to the here and now. De l'Épée paused for a moment before thrusting her hand through the square of darkness, but then she scrambled all the way up.

"Quickly, now," Janvier said, and he climbed as fast as he could while allowing Frémont to maintain his own contact.

Just as he had last night, Janvier pushed his way through the resistance, found the stone lip of the roof, and heaved himself over the edge under the glowing sky of a mysterious, alien world. He didn't waste any time on the scene or on talking to de l'Épée, who was gazing upward at the gigantic nebula, in rapt fascination, but turned and reached out to grasp Frémont's hand as soon as it emerged from the square of blackness. Janvier had been concerned the portal might close before Frémont was able to pass through, but either the timing was still good or else the portal was unable to fade with someone in transit, because it wasn't till the younger inspector had completed his ascent to the tower rooftop that it vanished as it had done the night before.

Frémont gazed speechlessly out at the ruined city, while de l'Épée had had a few moments more to take in the scene.

"Astonishing," she said. "Truly astonishing. I never would have imagined anything like this. Not in a million years."

"So," Janvier said. "That portal we came through is used up for today. According to what I was told, which may or may not be true, they only stay open for a few minutes following the stroke of midnight. Which means we should get a move on to the only other one I know of. You must have a million questions, and I have maybe two or three answers, but they can wait till we get back to our own city."

Nevertheless, Janvier took a moment to scan the city around the tower. Everything looked much the same as last night at first glance, the mysteriously illuminated white palace atop this world's Butte de Mars looked the same as before, but wait—were those birds flying around the structure? Surely at this distance ... Janvier's gaze locked onto one of the little winged black dots, and as if he had focused a telescope on it, it seemed to zoom crazily towards him.

It wasn't a bird at all, but a mythical monster, a night-gaunt, a pitch-black humanoid two and a half meters tall with no face whatsoever, no eyes or nostrils or mouth even, and leathery wings sprouting from its back. As Janvier looked with appalled horror on this creature that he had always assumed was nothing more than a noxious fairy tale, it loomed closer and closer. Janvier felt like not just his gaze had been transported the kilometer or more to the distant palace, but his body had been as well. He tried to wrench himself away, but he was paralyzed with something more and less than terror. He couldn't move or react as the creature's long bony hand with its talon-tipped fingers reached out impossibly towards him and wrapped around his neck—

De l'Épée lashed out with a perfect savate fouetté kick, whipping her foot into the creature's chest, breaking its grip on Janvier. The creature might have been strong, but it seemed it wasn't all that heavy as her kick knocked the night-gaunt violently backwards; it tripped on the cornice of the tower and fell over the edge, disappearing from sight. The paralysis that had gripped Janvier vanished the moment the monster let go of him, so he rushed to the edge of the roof and looked down. The night-gaunt tried to fly as it fell, but it was too close to the tower wall and its left wing bashed into the hard stone, flipping it over, and by then it was too late. The creature struck the ground with a crunch audible from the roof, spasmed once with all its limbs jerking frantically, and lay still.

"What—what *was* that thing?" Frémont's voice was tense.

"I don't know," Janvier said. "I don't even know what just happened. What did you see, de l'Épée?"

"One moment you were gazing out at that weird palace on the butte, the next, this … *thing*, a night-gaunt, I suppose it was, was *right there* on the roof with us, grabbing your neck. I know it's impossible, but it seemed like you were *calling* it from the butte. It seemed to stretch towards us. Like the space between you and it warped, somehow."

"Right," Janvier said. "Lesson learned. No more looking at things. Let's go downstairs while we still have time tonight. The city layout is like ours, the parts that aren't rubble. We're heading for the Place des Lutins."

Frémont provided their light spell as they descended. Janvier was conscious now of his temerity in bringing his people into a place whose dangers he obviously didn't understand. Concerned about the timing and how long the other portal would remain open, he didn't pause to show the inspectors the bird-person skeleton.

They emerged from the tower into the little plaza, identical to last night except of course for the corpse of the night-gaunt. Janvier and Frémont were both inclined to shy away from the horrible thing, but de l'Épée made straight for it. She seemed fascinated by the creature and took a moment to drink it in visually before reaching out to feel its slender, elongated arms and legs, putting her hand over the blank black ovoid of its nonexistent face, and fingering its membranous wings. Finally, she gathered the whole carcass up in her arms for a moment before laying it back down in the street.

"Poor thing," she said. "It weighs less than forty kilos. Must have hollow bones."

"Poor thing?" Frémont exclaimed, astonished.

"Yes, well … I'd kill it a hundred times over to save the chief, but look at it … Isn't it pitiable?"

Janvier forced himself to look. He understood what de l'Épée was saying. Despite its hideous strength, the night-gaunt was frail and pathetic in death. He'd called it to it somehow, it had reached out for him, maybe just a reflex action, and now it was dead. It was his fault, really.

•   •   •

Actually night-gaunts really are *irredeemably vicious monsters, and servants of even worse masters, so I have to smile at Janvier and de l'Épée's soft-heartedness.*

•   •   •

"Yes," he said. "It *is* pitiable. But that doesn't mean you didn't do the right thing, and it doesn't mean I'm not grateful. That was a beautiful kick, de l'Épée. I didn't know you were a master of the art."

"Oh, well. I just practice a little on weekends. Sergeant Diop from the 3rd has a savate class at the Jardin des Lapins every Saturday. Now *he's* a real master. For me it was just a bit of faire du sport, you know? Till now."

They navigated as quickly as possible through the ruined city toward the square that corresponded to the Place des Lutins in Lutèce. No monsters, bird-people, or secretive master thieves accosted them along the way. As they neared their destination, Janvier had the unwelcome thought: what if le Chat Azur had already used the portal? They'd never be able to find another one by wandering around at random. He didn't look forward to a day in this horrible place with no food or water.

So it was with some real relief that Janvier spied first that crumbling wall he remembered, and then moments later the impossibly dark shadow that signified the portal.

"Ah! Hold hands, everyone, and let's not waste time."

They formed up again and approached the portal.

"Wait! What's that?" Frémont had spotted a small white pasteboard square on the ground near the broken wall. "A calling card?"

It was indeed one of le Chat Azur's cards. A hasty pencil scrawl on the back read, "Take care, Commissaire. There's danger here. That house is on Avenue de Marigny."

•   •   •

It's possible that some readers may be familiar with an even more exclusive and pretentious Avenue de Marigny in a different city, not an avenue of townhouses and mansions as in Lutèce but rather of palaces. A naive child once declared that someday he would live on that street, and when he grew older, he remembered his foolish boast.

7

THEY ENTERED THE PORTAL and proceeded through the music shop, then emerged onto Lutèce's Place des Lutins none the worse for wear.

"I don't know about you, chief," Frémont said, "but at this point in the evening, I urgently need a drink. That's l'Entracte just across the plaza, and it will still be open for an hour or so."

•　　•　　•

I remember a different Bar de l'Entracte in the 2nd arrondissement, not the 9th, but this one has just as glorious a history. Good choice, Frémont!

•　　•　　•

"What do you think, de l'Épée?"

The older inspector nodded. "I am in total agreement, Commissaire."

Janvier was no abstainer, but he usually restricted himself to only two or three drinks with a meal, and never went out drinking by preference. *(Another reason I mistrusted him at first. I prefer people who can let themselves go.)* Tonight, however, he was willing to make an exception to the rule, and so the three officers found themselves a table out in the plaza where they could be sure no one was listening in on their conversation.

Over l'Entracte's excellent calvados (Janvier splurged on VSOP), he recounted his previous night's adventure, and also, with a little hesitation, Commissaire Renault's ominous warning about the shadow minister.

"I don't know what to say, boss," Frémont wrinkled his forehead. "I thought I understood what the world was like, but it's like I took a step out of my house and fell off a cliff. Metaphysically speaking. What does all this mean?"

"I wish I knew," Janvier said. "Because le Chat Azur says they don't understand it, either, and the little they did tell me might not be right. But troubling as the mere existence of that other city is, what's even worse for me is thinking that there must be other people here who are in on the secret. Because the thief didn't discover the other city. They found their way there by following someone else, so they said. And that means there's someone else who decided not to let the public know. Why is that? Who are these conspirators? Shouldn't we all have been told about that place, shouldn't we be exploring it, or if it's dangerous, shouldn't we be taking steps to protect the people of Lutèce? The very idea of that other city being such a secret disgusts me."

"Ugh. I understand what you mean," de l'Épée said. "But to be honest, I'm surprised that you told *us* about it so readily."

"I thought about it for a while," Janvier said. "I only hesitated because knowledge of this place seems likely to be a dangerous possession. But I realized if I held it back from you two, I'd be as bad as the secret-keepers. In fact, the only reason I haven't reported it all officially is that I'm afraid some of our brass might be in on the conspiracy. I've told one other person so far. You've met my mother. She's in the Scarlet Order at the university. A high-energy magic researcher. She says she never heard of any of this before either."

"I have to admit I'm frightened," Frémont said. "But despite what Commissaire Renault advised you, I'd feel a lot worse pretending none of this happened than trying to get to the bottom of it. Regardless of the danger."

Janvier looked at his subordinate, the pretty young man in the spring-colored suit. He'd never heard him so determined before. It was like he'd been hiding something beneath that dandyish exterior.

"I agree," de l'Épée said. "That's how I feel too. I'm not sure what our best course of action is, but I'm pretty sure we have to do *something*."

"Good." Janvier took a sip of his calvados. He didn't drink a lot of spirits, but he had to admit the stuff felt good on the way down. "Now, let's discuss our next steps. Arresting le Chat Azur is no longer a priority for me. But finding them is. Unfortunately, we have no idea where our thief is, or even which world they're in. And I don't want to abandon our watch over the baron's tower, because it would be a breach of orders and might give the game away. So, I'm going back there tonight. In the meantime, though, if you two can snatch a few spare hours ..."

"Explore Avenue de Marigny for anything interesting, right boss?" Frémont was eager to have something to do.

"Yes. I'll want a list of all owners and their addresses up and down the street. Needless to say, you're not to do anything intrusive that would upset any of those esteemed, respectable, and coincidentally ultra-rich and politically influential people. But there's also the summit of the Butte de Mars to look into, since it's so blatantly interesting in the other world. Isn't there a little park at that location in our city?"

"I think so," de l'Épée said. "I'll check it out."

"Thank you! One more thing. Under no circumstances go through any portals you may find. Not that they should be visible this long after midnight if le Chat Azur was telling the truth, but that's plainly not something to do on your own."

The squad's agreement this time was even more vehement. They finished the bottle, agreed to check in regularly using the police switchboard for urgent messages and the Tour des Corbeaux as a working headquarters. Janvier returned somewhat tipsily to the tower to astonish the door guard once again and to wait out another night.

•　　　•　　　•

Ninety-nine out of one hundred officers, even the most dutiful in a force known for its diligence, would have found a way to fall asleep for the remainder of the graveyard shift at the Tour des Corbeaux. The sleep-debt, the emotional stress of the past two days, the alcohol, the sheer tedium of doing an unobserved job that was known to be pointless ... you or I would certainly have succumbed. You might perhaps have been repentant when awakened; I would not. But our paragon Janvier, yawning hugely, was the hundredth; he remained awake the whole time. Unbelievable, I grant you, but he managed it, somehow. Whether he was trying to work out what was going on in his suddenly mysterious city or whether he was indulging in lurid fantasies regarding cat-clawed thieves pricking his bottom I can't say, however.

•　　　•　　　•

The night passed uneventfully, and Frémont dutifully arrived at 6:00 AM to relieve him.

"Here's the list of Avenue de Marigny property owners." Frémont handed over a notepad page. "Some of the oldest noble families in the city. No nouveau riche allowed. Unfortunately, I didn't see anything unusual from the street. All the smaller homes were quiet on a weekday night, and the ones with private grounds were all closed. I'd be more than happy to, let us say, find signs of suspicious activity on someone's estate and investigate if any of these names intrigue you."

"I'd rather you didn't get yourself fired," Janvier said, smiling through his yawn. He scanned the list of names and street numbers, a smaller subset of the ones he'd compiled yesterday. Many were known to him due to the family's prominence, but none leapt out as especially significant.

Leaving Frémont to continue what he supposed would be the pointless protection of Baron Corbeau's collection, Janvier returned home. 7:00 AM. No messages for him at headquarters. This time he managed a more substantial sleep, interrupted at 1:00 PM by the ringing phone.

"Commissaire? De l'Épée here. I looked into that matter you asked me to and found something interesting. Not urgent, but interesting."

Janvier smiled at her carefully elliptical phrasing. "Thank you. Let's meet at two to talk it over."

"Yes, sir. I'll see you then."

Janvier stopped at Les Tasses d'Antan to grab a croissant (somewhat stale this late in the day, but still good) and a coffee then headed for the tram that would take him to the Tour des Corbeaux.

He was walking towards the stop, among dozens of other pedestrians on the Boulevard des Cigognes, an extra-wide street planted with rows of stately elm trees. The world froze and turned monochrome. Janvier was frozen too, motionless, so immobile it was like he didn't have a body anymore, didn't have a heartbeat or a breath.

"What do you think you're doing, Commissaire?" The voice came from nowhere in particular. It was a plummy, self-satisfied voice, perhaps a middle-aged man's, but Janvier thought it had a curious slurring sense to it, even though the words were clear enough, like the speaker was half-asleep.

Even without a working mouth or lungs, Janvier found he could speak. "Pardon me?"

"Oh, don't play coy. I can see you. I can see everything. Anything to do with Baron Corbeau interests me, so I've been paying you special attention of late. And yet ..."

Janvier didn't answer. He didn't recognize his own feelings at the time, but he was transcendently angry at this invasion of his life and the overturning of his understanding of the world. If the owner of the voice had been physically present, he might well have resorted to violence for the first time in his life.

"And yet," the voice continued, "when I went to look last night, I couldn't find you at all. Do you care to explain yourself, Commissaire?"

"I owe you no explanation."

"Ha! Brash! I like it. Toujours l'audace, eh? But the curious thing is you actually do owe me, without knowing of the debt."

Another remark that didn't seem to require a response. "I suppose you must be the notorious shadow minister?"

"Indeed I am, my boy. Indeed I am. And as you must be aware, you are quite in my power. Do you feel no fear for your own safety? I could wipe you off the face of Lutèce, and no one would even know you were gone."

"It's unfortunate you can't see me shrugging," Janvier said. It was true, though, in his current state of mind, he really didn't care. He had no fear whatsoever, only anger. "My only obligation is to the people of Lutèce. When I was made a commissaire, I swore an oath to do my utmost to protect the city—"

The voice interrupted. "What a coincidence! So did I. And I'm quite the fan of yours, too, Commissaire, though you may not credit it. That business with the Butcher of Mars two years ago. Bad. Very bad. I still don't see why I didn't—But never mind. What I mean to say is I am fond of you, Janvier. Which is why I am having this conversation with you instead of—instead of taking other measures."

"It's not much of a conversation so far."

"Now, now, there's a point at which audacity gives way to mere rudeness. I'm giving you an opportunity to explain your actions."

"Go fuck yourself."

Janvier experienced the shadow minister's rage as if it was a physical tide of emotion, but he stood against it and after a moment the tide receded. The world unfroze, recolored itself, and Janvier's consciousness returned to his body. His memory of the conversation had been erased, and there was no physical evidence of anything unusual but he was aware nevertheless that something odd had just transpired that he couldn't quite pin down.

Janvier arrived at the Tour des Corbeaux without further incident. It had occurred to him that the moment of discontinuity he'd suffered on the street was rather like the jarring transition between worlds, but of course it was broad daylight and he hadn't passed through any portal. Still, the reflection gave him pause: what if he was in another world at this very moment? How could he ever be sure? When he rang the bell at the front door and was met by de l'Épée and Frémont his doubts vanished, however.

"Chief! It's good to see you." Frémont was effusive. "You'll definitely want to hear Jeanne-Marie's report."

"Indeed? What have you found out?"

They walked together through the tower's foyer into the ground-story hall and started up the stairs toward the gallery floors.

"Something interesting," de l'Épée said. "I explored the Jardin de Nuit this morning, which is what the little park at the top of the butte is called. It's not much of a park, some overgrown benches facing a strip that must have been a cultivated garden at some point but is now only brambles, a tangled grove of lindens, and a sandy terrain the locals use for games of boules. It's a crown property so the city administration doesn't maintain it, but the royals seem to have forgotten it's theirs.

"Anyway, it doesn't look like much. No one was there at that time of day except for a few pensioners taking their constitutionals, but I happened to walk close to the linden grove because I thought there might be something at its center. It turns out there's an old gazebo that you'd have to climb through a lot of shrubbery to get to, it's totally overgrown. But that's not the main thing: when I tried to push my way close to it, I felt this odd sensation, like a weaker form of that strange chill we got when we approached the portal in the tower. And as soon as I remembered what that was like it started to get dark. Just like last night. But no portal appeared."

Frémont and de l'Épée were looking at him expectantly.

"Interesting. It seems that the initiation notion le Chat Azur told me about is real. Perhaps a portal will open on the butte at midnight. I wonder ... you ought to be able to feel the same thing upstairs, right? And at that music shop in the Place des Lutins."

Frémont said, "I wanted to go try it out immediately, but she convinced me to wait for you, boss."

"I didn't want to provoke the baron's questions in your absence," de l'Épée said. "I wasn't sure what I'd tell him seeing as he'd asked us specifically not to disturb him on the top floor."

"Prudent," Janvier said. "But at this point I am less and less inclined to care about what Baron Corbeau thinks of us or to worry about any complaint he may file. Speaking of the baron, has he bothered either of you over the last day or so? Last time I saw him was yesterday morning."

"Not since you mention it, sir," de l'Épée said, and Frémont shook his head. "Me neither, chief."

"Strange. I would have expected him to be more annoying. And what is he doing up there, anyway? Let's go find him. That will give us a chance to test your discovery."

They went upstairs. Last night he had had to focus deliberately on the strange sensations and had only detected them fairly close to the trap door. But this time, even on the stairs of the middle stories of the tower he felt a touch of those chills down the spine, and when he focused on the sensation, the stairwell grew noticeably darker. As an experiment, Janvier tried to push the awareness of the phenomenon away and this caused the darkness and chills to recede until they weren't perceptible anymore except as a slight prickling sensation on the back of his neck.

"I feel it too," he whispered. "Excellent work, de l'Épée."

They proceeded upstairs, where Janvier rapped on the door of the baron's office and raised his voice. "Baron Corbeau? Are you there? It's Commissaire Janvier."

No answer. He must certainly have been audible in all the rooms of the floor. For decency's sake he waited a minute and tried the bedroom, but there was no response.

"You don't suppose—" began Frémont.

"I don't," Janvier said. "He couldn't have used the portal. We've used it ourselves for two nights running, and it's supposed to take all day to regenerate."

"Oh, right. But then—"

"It's possible he simply left the usual way through the front door during the period after midnight when we were in the other world. But before looking into that ..."

Janvier opened the office door. It was the same cluttered room he'd visited two days before, with no obvious changes since then. He moved back to the bedroom and opened the door.

"Oh."

The baron's bedroom was large and almost as cluttered as his office, but what drew Janvier's attention was the torn curtain, the shattered wooden shutters, and the twisted iron bars wrenched from the open window. He felt the urge to run to the window and look down, and Frémont obviously did as well, but after taking a step, the younger man hesitated even before Janvier could reach out and hold him back.

"Yes. Take care. This is a crime scene. Richard, check with the officer at the front door. Find out when they last saw the baron. If they haven't seen him at all, then you'll have to notify headquarters. Insist on speaking with Lambert personally, and if he's not there, don't tell anyone else. But if he's there, let Lambert know we're already investigating. And when you're done with Lambert, speak with Dr. Bernard and tell her to come. We'll need her analysis of the scene."

As Frémont ran downstairs, Janvier said, "de l'Épée, I'm relying on you for observations. I'll follow you around the room taking notes of what you find."

"Yes, chief."

On his promotion to commissaire, Janvier had indulged himself with the purchase of a fancy leather-bound notebook with an attached pencil. He produced it now and flipped to the first blank page, noting the date and time at the top.

De l'Épée began reciting, "First observations, from outside the bedroom of Baron Corbeau. Eighth and highest story of the Tour des Corbeaux. Approximately eight meters across, not square, but close enough. Salient observation, the broken window, with the curtain partially torn off the rod, the iron bars that formerly guarded the window twisted and broken, several ... four of them on the floor. The inner wooden shutter is shattered; part of it hangs open and the rest is in pieces, also on the floor. The window is large enough to allow a person to pass in or out. Observation: it looks like force was applied from the outside to burst through the bars and the shutter."

She paused between remarks, allowing Janvier time to take the notes; he grunted when he was ready and she took a few steps into the room, carefully avoiding treading on any debris or touching anything with her hands. Janvier followed just behind her.

"I am proceeding into the baron's chamber. The room is full of books and curios, but most of it appears to be in good order except for the area around the bed and the window. Approaching the bed ..."

It was the same iron frame piece as in the other city, though here it was in much better shape, not rusty or dilapidated. Janvier suffered another frozen moment of what he had begun to think of as philosophical horror. Naming the sensation did nothing to lessen its effect. How could it possibly be the same bed? He had no explanation to grasp at, and the inexplicability of the situation made him feel a bit faint.

"Sir?" de l'Épée had noticed his start.

Janvier caught hold of himself. "Carry on, de l'Épée. I'll explain when you're done."

"Very well. The bedclothes are in disarray, partially on the floor, but I can't say whether they were disturbed by a sleeper, presumably Baron Corbeau, or by an intruder. It's clear the bed was occupied, however, as there is the definite impression on the undersheet of the sleeper's body. Ah!"

"What?"

"I think—yes, I'm fairly confident, though we'll have to wait for Dr. Bernard to be certain. A blood stain. Not a dangerous quantity, perhaps a few CCs, but more than would ever spill from a mere scratch. Dry now, but not yet turned black. I'd say less than a day old, but I could easily be wrong."

De l'Épée looked carefully at the bed without touching it, then moved on toward the window, pausing to scrutinize the floor and then the walls near the window.

"There are a few more drops of blood on the floor here, between the bed and the window, consistent with a wound made on the bed and subsequent movement toward the window. No sign of a fight taking place as nearby shelves are in good order and it would be difficult to fight without knocking things over in this cluttered room. However, the baron was an elderly man and if surprised asleep he might have been unable to resist an intruder."

Now she approached the window.

"The window frame is largely intact, but on the wooden sill that remains from the shutter assembly I see several deep gouges. I'm going to try the remaining bar."

De l'Épée pulled up the fabric of her tweed jacket to avoid touching the bar with bare skin and gripped it firmly. Then she set her feet and pulled.

"The bar I tried is deeply embedded in the stone. I can't budge it by hand. But four of these two-centimeter-thick bars were wrenched entirely out of their sockets. Observation: extreme strength or considerable time using tools with purchase would have been required to do this. Commissaire, would you brace me? I want to look out the window without touching anything."

Janvier held onto de l'Épée as she awkwardly angled herself through the broken window to look outside.

"Thank you. There are gouges in the stone just outside the window. Looking down I see nothing on the wall below, however, and nothing unusual in the street. Nothing up above either, or on the roof."

At this point Frémont returned, breathless from running up eight flights of stairs. "The officer downstairs is certain the baron never left. I called headquarters and got through to the inspecteur-general. I hardly had time to tell him anything at all before he cut me off. Lambert said to make sure this is kept absolutely quiet for now, no talking to anyone else about the case, but that's all he said. Dr. Bernard is on her way."

"Well done. In the novels I read, the detective never speculates, only explains what actually happened when they're certain. But I suppose you know what this looks like to me, right?"

De l'Épée nodded. "Night-gaunt. Now that we know they actually exist. It's obvious there was an intrusion here, through the window. Something strong enough to break the iron bars, something that could fly. Something big enough to carry off the baron, or his body. Not a hundred percent certain, but come on. What else could have done this?"

"Right," Janvier said. "We're not certain, but this is the only explanation that makes sense. A team of master thieves who deliberately simulated entry in this absurd manner? A brutally strong sorcerer who somehow came up with a personal flight spell despite no one at the university having figured one out? Nonsense. There may be other explanations, but of the ones we have at hand a night-gaunt is the only one that I can think of, especially considering we know there's a portal here. Not that it should have been possible for the creature to use it, but perhaps it came through a different one, perhaps it was attracted to the tower because of the portal here … That's just speculation. What do you think, Frémont?"

The younger inspector had caught his breath. "I agree, boss. It's just … I have a hard time thinking this was random. No one has ever seen a night-gaunt in Lutèce before. And even though it may have been strong enough to break through the window and carry the baron off, why would it go to the trouble? In the old stories that's what they do, carry people off, but there must have been people on the street it could much more easily have grabbed. It took a lot of effort to break in here. So I have to think …" He trailed off, as if unwilling to express the thought.

"You think it was sent?" Janvier nodded. "That's plausible, for just the reasons you stated. However even if we're right about what happened, our understanding of why is weaker, so while the idea of it being sent to snatch Baron Corbeau feels right to me, it's not something we can just run with without more evidence. You understand what I'm saying?"

"Yes, boss. And anyway we have no idea who would want to commit this crime or where the creature may have flown off to. Not yet, anyway. And I presume we don't want to speculate about this possibility to the inspecteur-general, either."

"No. Because making people disappear is what the shadow minister is supposed to do."

"There is one thing that *does* come to mind, though," de l'Épée said. "A night-gaunt … in the city. Suppose someone sees it flying around? We can check the logbook at the arrondissement station in case someone reports it, and also the curiosity columns in the papers."

"Good idea."

"Oh, Boss," Frémont added, "I nearly forgot. The officer out front, she says neither she nor her partner heard any sound or disturbance from the tower during their entire watch. We can check with the arrondissement to make sure because the crime may have occurred in another pair's shift, but doesn't it seem strange they wouldn't have noticed anything at all? You'd think wrenching these iron bars out of the stone and breaking through the shutters would have been loud enough to hear, even thirty meters up."

"Hm. Yet another mystery. But it's a good point. When you have some free time—if you ever do, anyway—check in with Inspector Delameter at the 9th station, just to be sure."

8

IT WASN'T HALF AN HOUR BEFORE Dr. Bernard arrived with her worn satchel full of instruments and sample containers. The doctor was dressed in a healer's black silk tunic and trousers with a blue uniform police cape over her shoulders. Janvier remembered her diligent work during the Butcher of Mars aftermath. She'd impressed him with her professionality as well as her imperturbability, analyzing the crime scene and cataloging the murderer's gruesome trophies. It had been Dr. Bernard who had noticed how traumatized young inspector Janvier had been back then and she who recommended that he seek therapy for his nightmares.

"Commissaire," she said. "I won't say it's a pleasure in the circumstances, but it's good to work with you again on a case. Sounds like quite the situation."

"Yes, Doctor. I'm curious what you make of all this. We've touched nothing with bare hands and hardly disturbed the scene at all."

"Good. I should wait for the photographer to arrive before proceeding."

"Not this time. No photos."

Dr. Bernard raised an eyebrow but said nothing. She set to work. Her preliminary survey took only a quarter hour; in addition to minute study of the same evidence de l'Épée had discovered, she cast a few spells using a purple monocle as an accessory.

"The blood here was most likely spilled soon after midnight," she said. "A minor wound at worst. Even without treatment the subject would probably be just fine if that was the only injury suffered. I've dusted out some of these curious gouges in the stone but you'll have to wait for the lab work before I find out if there's anything useful there. Same for the bedclothes and the analysis of the bloodstain, which I'll have to bring back to the Quai des Serpents with me, but I'm reasonably confident it's human. No sorcery has been cast in this room for at least 24 hours, but I have some odd indications from the Apterbach test. It's possible some enchanted object has been in this room more recently, but nothing magical is present right now."

"Enchanted object?"

"Or someone with a powerful spell previously cast operating on their person," Dr. Bernard said. "A spell of stealth, for example, to suppress the sound of the break-in. Though that's mere speculation."

"I see. Thank you, Doctor. I'm sure the scene has impressed you with its strangeness. I know you'd never discuss your findings with anyone outside the force, but I want to caution you that even within the Police Judiciaire you should use extreme discretion."

•   •   •

Needless to say, Janvier was suffering agonies just then as he wanted to tell her everything, but he'd been reflecting on the danger the shadow minister seemed to present and decided it would be kinder not to burden the doctor with either his knowledge or his speculations.

•   •   •

"Ah. It's one of *those*, is it?" Dr. Bernard nodded once, sharply. "I understand, Commissaire. Thank you for the warning."

She put him somewhat at ease with the suggestion that she understood the danger. This made him wonder just how many people in the police and elsewhere in the city had at least some inkling of the shadow minister's influence, and how long he might have been allowed to blithely continue in his position as a senior police officer without any such hints for himself.

The doctor said, "I suppose there's no need for me to discuss the implications of the physical evidence. I've never seen anything like this before, but the idea of something being able to burst through these bars—well. I'll be done with the lab work in a few hours."

•   •   •

Dr. Bernard having departed with her samples, Janvier and his officers reconvened in the baron's gallery to discuss their next steps, blobby expressionist figures looking over their shoulders from the canvases.

"What's the plan for midnight, Boss?" Frémont wanted to know.

"The plan is to do absolutely nothing with these portals till further notice." Janvier hoped he sounded convincing. "We can't go wandering around monster-infested ruins on our own. At least without any sensible goal. It's true the baron is in danger, and maybe the thief is too, but we need a better idea where they are before we go haring off after them. And both of them could well be in our city, not the other world."

Frémont looked like he wanted to argue, but he held his tongue.

"I know it's hard to sit on our hands," Janvier said. "But if you have any ideas, they should be for things we can do here in Lutèce."

"Question, sir."

"Yes, de l'Épée?"

"If we knew that a particular house on the Avenue de Marigny was of interest, would that be enough for us to proceed? Either to investigate the homeowner as a suspect, or to look for a portal on the grounds?"

"Quite possibly." Janvier saw where she was headed. "But I can't ask you to risk your careers. What are you thinking, some kind of ruse?"

"Well, yes."

Janvier saw that Frémont wasn't following. He mimed pressing a doorbell, bowed, and pretended to offer his card to an imaginary butler.

"Is Vicomte Bonhomme at home? I'd like to talk to him about this year's donation to the police community fund."

Frémont said, "Oh! I see."

"To gain some freedom of the grounds, perhaps you have to use the toilet or perhaps you admire the architecture or ask about the gardens and they can hardly refuse to show you around. And then you can use this creepy portal-detection sense we've acquired to identify the right house."

Janvier shook his head. "The problem will come when Vicomte Bonhomme with his million a year income and his buddies in the ministry discovers there is no police community fund drive. And when Lambert hears we've been harassing the sort of people he likes to pander to. I might possibly escape with a severe dressing-down, but it would be your career if you annoy the wrong noble."

"Commissaire, if I may?" De l'Épée again.

"Of course."

"Speaking just for myself," she said, "*fuck* my career. And fuck the inspecteur-general, too. I'd rather be fired for trying to save someone's life and for trying to uncover the truth of what's going on in this city than keep my head down like Renault advised us."

"I feel the same way, sir," Frémont said.

"You understand it's not just our brass and administrative punishment we have to worry about. It's the shadow minister, too."

"That changes nothing for me, sir. As far as I'm concerned, if the shadow minister even exists, they're just another criminal."

"If that's how you feel, then we're in for it, now. Frémont, I bet you're behind on sleep, so I want you to grab a few hours, but when you find some time you can start on the good householders of the Avenue de Marigny. Start on the north end of the avenue and we'll take the south. I'm afraid de l'Épée and I will find our own time occupied for a while at headquarters going through the administrative motions for the baron's case, depending how far Lambert wants us to proceed with it. Use the switchboard for messages as usual, but we'll also meet back here at ten again to confer."

•   •   •

"I'm going to be a bit obtuse during this meeting," Janvier told de l'Épée as they rode the tram back to headquarters. At this time of day, early afternoon, the tram wasn't crowded, just a few shoppers on board returning from their errands. "To find out what's what. It's possible this case will be handled with the usual formalities, but I'm guessing not. You'll be with me as a sort of preventive measure."

"Sir?"

"I've been thinking about this. If Lambert wants to suppress the investigation, or keep it quiet, he'll have to instruct me to do so. And that's his right. But he might go further than that, and I don't want to hear him out if he does. I have to obey orders, or at least acknowledge them, but I'd rather not be made an accomplice, if you see what I mean."

"Ah! And if I'm there, he'll be less inclined to be indiscreet. Is it wise to provoke him, though?"

"Probably not. But if he were to suggest something grossly improper in the interests of politics or worse, in submission to some shadow minister bogey-man, I'd have to go public or resign or some such dramatic thing. I want to keep my job until we've rescued our victim, or at least discovered his fate."

"Understood. I'll just stand there with my mouth shut, then."

•   •   •

With de l'Épée in tow, Janvier knocked on Lambert's office door. They'd been met at the entrance to headquarters by an aide who'd told them they were wanted upstairs immediately.

"Enter," came Lambert's voice, so they walked inside. The inspecteur-general's office was five times as large as Janvier's with modern furniture, a coffee machine on a sideboard, and a cubby for his secretary, currently unoccupied. Lambert gestured for Janvier to draw up a chair and sit down. De l'Épée remained standing by the door.

The inspecteur-general shot a quick glance at de l'Épée, as if he preferred she weren't there, but though he could have asked her to leave he only said, "Ah. Janvier. Bad business, this. But then that's your job, isn't it? Dealing with bad business."

"Yes, sir. A very disturbing crime, I must say. Have a public prosecutor and an examining magistrate[4] been assigned yet? I'm eager to get the case properly under way."

"Ha-hm." Lambert steepled his fingers and looked down at them as if to find some insight. "Not yet, Janvier. We're still not quite certain as to the nature of the crime, are we? For the matter of that, it's not even certain a serious crime has been committed at all. We wouldn't want to look like fools before the courts."

---

[4] These two officials are assigned by the court system early in a criminal investigation, often even before a suspect has been identified. They usually don't have much work to do until the arrest, however. The examining magistrate is formally in charge of the case, but the police generally perform the investigation themselves.

"Of course not, sir. So if I understand you, sir, you wish me to proceed discreetly for now, with no official case docketed."

"Exactly." Lambert glanced at de l'Épée. He sighed and shook his head without saying anything more except to mutter "Bad business," again.

"Have we notified the baron's surviving relations? His friends and business associates? He must have an attorney, at least."

"He was the last of his line," Lambert said. "Quite the hermit, I'm told, but I don't know much more than that. I'm not aware of a lawyer, but you may be able to find one by canvassing Maîtres' Row. If no heir is found the tower will no doubt revert to the crown. For now, though, you mustn't let on that he's disappeared. You'll need to come up with some other excuse for your inquiry."

"Just so, sir. Discretion. Now then, about le Chat Azur. I suppose the 9th arrondissement had better continue to guard the baron's tower. But it's hard to believe a League thief would perform a violent break-in, much less an assault and kidnapping or murder. I think I must expand the scope of my investigation to include other suspects."

Lambert looked like he wanted to object but he hesitated before answering with obvious reluctance. "As you see fit, Commissaire. It's your investigation. You have full authority."

•　　•　　•

Outside again, Janvier wiped his forehead; he really had been sweating, too. "I hated every second of that," he told de l'Épée. "Full authority! Full responsibility if anyone blames the police is what he meant."

"But you were brilliant," she said. "Didn't give anything away, didn't flout his orders, but also didn't ask questions about the oddness of keeping the case unofficial, and made it clear you weren't open to influence, either."

"Your presence was extremely helpful. My goal was to be too stupid to be subtly swayed, and you made it impossible for him to come out and make anything explicit. He must have been too afraid of appearances to ask you to leave. But did you notice the most salient feature of that little scene?"

"Yes. Rather shocking, really. We were there because Lambert requested it, and yet he didn't actually ask you anything. All he did was answer your questions. And he seemed rather relieved when it was over too."

"Yes. Like he wanted to wash his hands of it. And in particular Lambert didn't ask about the crime scene. Anyone would have been interested in such a strange occurrence, much less the head of Criminal Investigations. Also, the crime must have occurred while I was supposed to be on duty at the tower, and he didn't point that out either. Either he's complicit, which honestly I can't believe, or more likely he regards this case as a hot potato and is trying to avoid any dangerous knowledge that might come his way. There's no one who could have given him details about the crime scene before us apart from Dr. Bernard, and I doubt he's ever spoken two words to her."

De l'Épée shrugged. "We can find out easily enough. Perhaps she's discovered something useful from her analysis."

•   •   •

The doctor was gratifyingly concise when they went upstairs to her lab on the fifth floor. She ticked off points from her notebook.

"Bedclothes stain confirmed as human blood, type AB. Shed soon after midnight last night. I checked with the Guilde des Guérisseurs; Baron Corbeau has never donated blood nor undergone any blood work, so his type is unknown."

Janvier frowned. More evidence of the baron's strangeness. Everyone in Lutèce donated blood regularly.

She flipped a page.

"Gouges in the tower wall yielded a mix of powdery material; most of it basalt from the wall itself, but there were traces of limestone as well, as if whatever had gouged the basalt had recently been used on another stone surface. Of course, almost all the architectural stonework in Lutèce is limestone, but the vast majority is creamy gray. This stone, however, is almost white, which is quite rare in the city."

"Ah," Janvier said. "That's helpful."

"I'm happy to hear it," Dr. Bernard said, "because I'm afraid that's about all I've uncovered. The bedclothes had been recently cleaned and hadn't picked up anything but the usual bits of dead skin and a few hairs, all of which appear to be the baron's. Other fragments and dust on the floor were from the room and the casement as expected."

On the way out of the lab de l'Épée and Janvier turned to one another and said "The otherworld palace," and "That place on the butte," simultaneously. De l'Épée gestured for Janvier to speak first.

"Ha, yes. The monster probably came from the other city. That's reassuring and distressing at the same time."

De l'Épée nodded. "Let me guess. Reassuring because it means we don't have an unknown nest of night-gaunts in our city, distressing because it means one of them was able to travel to our world on its own."

"Or it was sent, even worse. But we can't do much about it for now, either way, not unless it's sighted somewhere in the city. For now, we have the thief's note to deal with."

"Yes, sir."

"You take the left side of Avenue de Marigny, and I'll take the right, heading up the street from the south. We'll probably see Frémont coming down from the north eventually. If we don't meet by chance on the street we can always convene back at the Tour des Corbeaux at ten."

•　　　•　　　•

No streets in Lutèce were ugly. There were no slums within the city limits, and no surrounding shantytown of the impoverished. Even the industrial districts were clean, well-kept, and pleasant to the eye. But Avenue de Marigny, the most exclusive street in Lutèce, was the city's ne plus ultra.

Tall, shady elms lined the broad sidewalks, while the exquisitely landscaped expanses of the only private lawns in the city radiated aristocratic elegance and pretension. Every cobblestone had its place and every polished brass gaslamp had its mantle replaced at the slightest sign of deterioration. The sequence of stately, manorial townhouses and their gravel and fieldstone drives was relieved from time to time by quaint épiceries, Esperian and Almany delicatessens, and some of the fanciest vintners in the city.

After an hour spent visiting the first three houses on the street, Janvier had collected well over 10,000 livres in pledges for the police community fund. He resolved to find out what the proper charity was actually called and deliver the cheques personally if he still had a job when all this was over. The problem had turned out not to be wangling access, but in finding a way to decently leave without gross impoliteness.

He'd received two extensive tours of exquisitely elegant townhouse-mansion interiors and lovely outside gardens in full bloom and had actually been asked to dinner by the third noble host, who hoped to show him off to her salon. But Janvier had detected no hint of any eldritch darkness, felt no strange chills thrilling their way down his spine, and not a single shadow of a high-flying night-gaunt had crossed his path. He calculated he had at least a dozen houses to visit, maybe more, before he crossed paths with Frémont working his way down the street from the other end. De l'Épée had not appeared, so she must still be investigating one of the houses across the street.

Then came the fourth house, the largest grounds yet, ten hectares surrounded by high hedges whose tops were worked into amazing topiary forms. The main gate was a fantasy in gilded iron. A discreet little placard by the left upright read "Sans Souci" in ornate green letters enameled onto a white background.

Now, where had he recently seen something like that before? He couldn't quite put his finger on it, but then he remembered at least part of it: Sans Souci was the residence of the most famous libertine in a city noted for its pleasures, the fabulously wealthy Chevalier Armand l'Étranger, chief patron of the Guilde du Plaisir. Of course, many wealthy persons in Lutèce competed for pride of place in supporting the courtesans' guild, but l'Étranger was widely acknowledged to be the guild's preeminent sponsor. His quarterly "nocturne" fêtes that often employed dozens of guild members at a time were some of the most sought-after invitations in Lutèce.

No staff were present at the gate or visible just inside the grounds, so Janvier shrugged and walked on in, following the flagstone path through the lush green lawn to a large circular marble fountain that featured a winged youth sculpted in gold offering a shimmering cascade of water from one outstretched hand. Janvier would have supposed it a mere artistic fantasy a few days before, but now he wondered if the statue was from life. The path continued between parallel rows of gorgeously blossoming rose bushes to the door of the ornate three-story mansion, which had been fashioned in the Esperian manner with a broad portico and elegantly curved granite stairs leading up to the entrance. If any home in Lutèce was to remain closed to him, Janvier thought, this was probably the one. On the other hand, if he *was* admitted, how Frémont would eat his heart out at not having had the chance himself!

Janvier pulled the bell-cord with its golden handle and heard a corresponding chime resonating from somewhere deep within the mansion. He waited a full minute and was just about to leave when the door opened.

"Yeeees?"

Janvier turned back to face the most exquisitely beautiful person he'd ever seen, a man with shimmering pale blue skin and a long mane of blue-blond hair. He was nude beneath an open silk house-gown in pink and gold, and carried himself not with the unselfconscious casualness of a naturist nor the defiant brashness of an exhibitionist, but rather with the self-aware bearing of a performer who knows full well he has mastered his performance and his audience as well. After boggling for an embarrassingly long moment, Janvier realized this could only be the master courtesan Kefildur, the very water elemental who Frémont had so dreamily described the day before.

•　　•　　•

A word about nudity in Lutèce, in case this account reaches readers brought up in prudery like those from the city in which I was born. Apart from the height of summer, nudity outdoors wasn't often very comfortable in temperate Lutèce, and so only the most determined naturists could be found unclothed except on exceptionally warm and sunny days (this was one, incidentally, a lovely and unseasonably warm day in late May). And since it was so inconvenient not to wear clothes on city streets, such brave persons would usually only be found disporting themselves in parks and at the seashore, usually with a change of clothes ready for their return home. Nudity at home was not uncommon during summertime leisure hours, and no one would be shocked to encounter an unclothed householder who didn't bother to put anything on before answering the door. At such a mansion as this, one would usually have expected a liveried butler or page to welcome guests, however. Even our straight-laced Janvier was more taken aback by the combination of the elemental's exotic appearance and their extraordinary beauty than by the fact of their partial nudity.

•　　•　　•

"Pardon me," Janvier said after another paralyzed moment. "I, er, I'm hoping to see Chevalier l'Étranger." He fumbled for his card and handed it over. "It's about, um, the police community fund."

"Commissaire Jules Janvier? Our city's savior? The chevalier is indisposed, but for my own part I'm delighted to receive you! I am Kefildur."

"Enchanté. But you're exaggerating. I hardly—"

"But no! Had you not apprehended that ... that monster, who knows but that your people's beautiful dream, this lovely city ... it might have fallen, fallen entirely to terror!"

Janvier wanted to protest that the elemental was grossly inflating the importance of the criminal and his crimes, however dreadful they might have been. But Kefildur's words, suggesting the city falling, brought the ruined city of the other world unpleasantly to mind. Could it be that his Lutèce was so delicately balanced on the edge of ruin? Surely not. He snapped back to the here and now as Kefildur was still speaking.

"As one who has come to live among humans ... adopted a human body and chosen to follow the curious paths of human pleasure ... I should have been desolated to lose all of that. You have no idea how fearful I was during that dreadful time; how grateful I was to hear the news that you had finally ended the butcher's reign of terror! I remember thinking to myself, I remember—oh! And you're right here!"

The elemental raised his hand to Janvier's cheek, and Janvier stood there frozen, feeling the peculiar coolness of the elemental's touch, not daring to acknowledge it and yet finding it impossible to step away.

•   •   •

If you've been following along so far, you must know how unlike proper Janvier this is, how deeply affected he must be at this moment to entertain such intimacy at all, much less while on duty.

•   •   •

All at once, Janvier understood several things. The first of which was that he'd been lying to himself about not needing someone. In fact, he'd been desperate for the twin solaces of affection and intimacy these last two years. The second was Kefildur's secret identity, which revelation he now understood must have been entirely deliberate, because if the elemental cared to conceal it they could easily have done so.

Kefildur continued, speaking softly now that they were standing so close, "I remember thinking if only he was here before me, I would reward my hero the best way that I could, I would show him my gratitude. You being here now, it's a dream come true!"

Janvier knew this was, well, not *wrong*, exactly, not that, but a distraction from other more important matters. And yet the elemental's uncanny blue eyes were gazing into his own, just inches away, and their arms were around him, and they were kissing, and those cool lips pressing against his own were impossible to resist ...

The elemental asked, "This is what you want, too, isn't it?"

Janvier couldn't speak, his emotions were so high; he could only kiss Kefildur of his own accord in reply.

Kefildur led Janvier by the hand from the chevalier's front door back to the fountain and its statue. Under the pitiless gaze of that shining golden figure they embraced, and on that soft green lawn they lay down together while fine prickling points of spray fell all about them and rainbows shimmered in their eyes. Time itself was annihilated and Janvier died and was reborn, and when he came to himself an hour later he found he was crying, tears rolling down his face for no reason he could fathom.

•　　　•　　　•

A note on sorcery and consent may be necessary here, though I'm sorry to interrupt what I must say was some truly rhapsodic prose. I'm really at my best at such moments, don't you agree? But anyway, spells of arousal, enthrallment, and glamour were well known at this time in Lutèce, though their use was strictly forbidden without explicit mutual agreement. I don't want to give the impression that Kefildur used some illicit or sneaky means to seduce our friend Janvier. It's just that they really were that good at understanding human emotions, with all the special insight of a nonhuman who had put so much time and effort into studying us. They knew very well this was something Janvier wanted, but even so you'll note the fact that they took the time to confirm consent orally.

One of my early readers expressed concern that Janvier's anti-magic effect might harm Kefildur, who was after all an essentially magical being. To be precise, Janvier's personal aura had an anti-sorcery effect, considering sorcery as a particular patterned approach to magic consciously expressed through spells that make use of geometrically mathematical formulations. While Kefildur was also a sorcerer, their essential elemental magic was deeper and in a sense more primitive, and was not substantially affected by Janvier's unfortunate disability.

•   •   •

"Why?" asked the elemental, meaning "why are you crying?" but Janvier just shook his head, unable to answer. They were side by side on the grass. One hand stroking Janvier's belly, the elemental kissed Janvier's cheeks, lapping up his tears with his long blue tongue.

"Ah," Kefildur said a few moments later, as if drinking the tears had provided enlightenment. "I understand. The Butcher of Mars. Still, after all this time. That monster hurt you, didn't he? His very existence hurt you badly, as it did me. And then even after you stopped him, you realized your world was different from the one you had believed in ... Ah, yes. Who wouldn't be wounded? It's too bad, isn't it?"

Janvier found he had stopped crying. "What is?"

"Our world. It's not as ... as pure as we would like. But you know ..." (here the elemental lowered his hand to offer

Janvier a gentle, intimate caress) "... it's not all bad, either. It's worth saving what we can, isn't it?"

Their words sparked something in Janvier, deep inside, and from the sweet softness he had been feeling, from the delicious languor of rémanence, something hard and determined emerged.

●　　　●　　　●

No, that's <u>not</u> what I meant. Something metaphorically hard and determined!

●　　　●　　　●

"Yes," said Janvier. "Always. That's what we must do. Save what we can."

Janvier kissed Kefildur one more time and then he got to his feet, offering the elemental a hand up. "What you just did for me—what we did, I mean, it's too much for me to even talk about right now. Can we—" he hesitated, remembering Kefildur was a courtesan, a professional, and despite evidence to the contrary, he wondered, what if this was just ... mechanical for them? What if—

"Of course we can! There's a lot more we have to talk about, and a lot more love-making for us to do. This was so lovely, too, everything I'd dreamed of ... Don't you dare think this was just one-way."

"Oh, no!" Janvier hesitated. "Or rather, I *did* think it because I can't help it, but truly I know better." He started gathering up his clothes. "I really do want to speak to the chevalier, though. Is he here?"

"Yes. Indisposed, however. But maybe that's not the right word. There's something terribly wrong with him, and I'm worried, but he refuses to let me call anyone in to help. I've been taking care of him as best I can. But maybe.. maybe it would be for the best if you did something for him. Come with me. Worst comes to worst he can only throw us out."

•　　•　　•

Worst come to worst was like nothing Kefildur could have imagined, so it's just as well he didn't know better.

9

K EFILDUR ESCORTED JANVIER into the house. They walked through a large hall that in one of the other grand houses on Avenue de Marigny might have been a ballroom. At Sans Souci it had a different function, what with the pink gauze curtains softening the space, plush furniture, pillows and cushions everywhere and the erotic art adorning the walls. The lack of people in a place dedicated to orgies and erotic performances felt spooky. Kefildur said the chevalier had told the servants and other courtesans usually in attendance to go home.

"But he kept you on? And you stayed with him."

They were walking through a broad corridor with a rose-colored carpet down the center running over a parquet floor. Cherry wood wainscoting carved in an intricate floral fretwork lined the walls and rose-shaped brass fixtures concealed the gaslights. A pair of doors with an elaborate rose design in gold running between them so that the rose would split in two when the doors opened stood at the far end of the passage.

"He wanted me to leave him alone, too. But I ... I can't bear to abandon someone who needs me. I'm afraid he'll be angry when he realizes I've brought you. I'm breaking my word to let no one in to see him."

"When did he become like this?"

"He's been getting worse for a while," the elemental said. "At first he was just drinking too much. Lately he's been suffering from terrible spells of melancholy. But there was a crisis two days ago, when I stepped out for a while, and since then ... he's not in good shape. Perhaps I should have summoned a healer, but he ordered me not to. He didn't say anything about the police, though—Ah. Here we are. He's in ... I suppose you'd call this his boudoir. It's the next room out from his bedroom, anyway."

Janvier reached out to open the doors and the premonition of something terrible to come descended on him like a weighted blanket bearing him down. It wasn't a concrete fear but something nebulous, something with the odor of the Butcher of Mars about it, as if another ghastly chamber of horrors waited in the next room.

He hesitated with his hands on the handles concealed in the roses set into the twin doors. Entering now felt terribly intrusive, and far outside of his regular duty. Of course, Janvier had become suspicious about the location, and le Chat Azur had all but told him this was something he needed to look into. But if he had been on his own, he might not have persisted against the weight of the weird and the dread that threatened from within.

It was easy to rationalize turning away, too. In Lutèce people had the right to live and die as they saw fit. But for Kefildur's sake, even though their intimacy was only an hour old, Janvier was prepared to go far, far out of his way. And though the elemental was reluctant to explain, they were plainly distraught, deeply concerned for the chevalier, not just as a client, but as a friend and as a lover, too. Still, he thought, maybe he shouldn't ...

With a convulsive effort of will, Janvier threw open the doors. The room revealed was windowless, a smaller version of the orgy hall. L'Étranger's boudoir was wrapped in soft pinkness: pink arras, pink drapes softening the lines of the ceiling, pink cushions and overlapping rugs, all slightly different shades, but not clashing, rather contributing to a womblike sense of coziness and protection. Cabinets, dressers, and bureaus lined the walls, shrouded by sheer pink silks. And in the center, sitting on the floor and leaning up against a richly upholstered chaise longue, a blond man in a golden dressing gown, embroidered all over with red roses. His head was sagging against his chest, his legs were splayed out on the floor like a bear's, and he had one hand on the neck of a bottle on an adjacent low side-table.

"Oh good," Kefildur said quietly, "he's not having one of his spells."

Janvier had been expecting to find an elderly man, since the chevalier had been well-known in Lutèce for many years. He was surprised to see that l'Étranger's face was unlined and his skin was clear, if rather pale; he couldn't be older than forty.

"Armand! This is my friend Commissaire Janvier," the elemental said, raising his voice. "You remember, the hero of the butte."

Chevalier l'Étranger raised his head slowly, as if it were difficult for him.

"I don't know any Janvier," he said dully. "Didn't I tell you not to let anyone in?"

Janvier looked him in the eyes. Green irises. He'd never seen green eyes before. Human eyes in Lutèce ranged from a pale violet like Frémont's to de l'Épée's midnight-purple or else like Janvier's were tawny yellow.

"I'm sorry to trouble you, sir. I thought you might be in need of assistance. Is there anything I can do for you?"

L'Étranger chuckled. "I have all I need right here." He raised the brandy bottle. "I don't need your help either, Kefildur. Take your new boyfriend with you."

"Armand, I—"

L'Étranger cut him off. "Get out. For—For pity's sake. Just get out." His voice was more weary than angry.

Janvier had never heard that formula before, 'for pity's sake', and he wasn't sure what it even meant, but the chevalier's wishes were clear enough. He could sense the elemental wanted to argue, but he thought it would be futile and would only provoke l'Étranger further, so he put his hand on Kefildur's arm and guided him out of the room.

●　　●　　●

"All right," Janvier said, once the doors had closed on the chevalier. "Talk to me. Tell me what's going on. Why did you ask me to come here?"

"Me?"

"You left that note for me in the ruined city, directing me here."

"Oh. You figured it out." Kefildur sounded miserable.

Janvier took the elemental's hand between both of his, raised it to his mouth, and kissed it. Kefildur looked at him with tears welling up in his liquid blue eyes.

"Listen," Janvier said, "I just want to know, all right? I don't think there's anything you can do or say to change my mind about you. And I'm sure you wanted me to figure it out, too. I should have done so sooner."

"Really?"

"Come on now. Le Chat Azur. Ha! I mean, when an ondine who affects an azure-skinned body makes love to me out of the blue—sorry, that was unintentional—I could hardly avoid realizing the truth. Of course, an elemental can change their shape, but until I connected the dots that was pretty clever, appearing to me in such a different form at the tower."

Kefildur's form softened, melted, and a moment later, she—*they* were standing there, just as alluringly feminine as they had been in the cat suit the first time they met. Then, a moment later, they became a hermaphrodite, then a sexless epicene, at last reverting to the male body they'd been presenting to begin with.

"Just as beautiful in any form," Janvier said, smiling at them.

"Thank you. It took me years to achieve a realistic human body, and longer still to perfect my appearance. My appearances, I should say. I told myself when I was sneaking up on you that night at the tower, even if he arrests me it will be all right because it will be *Janvier* arresting me. I'd already fallen for you by then, you see, sight unseen."

"Did you realize I wanted you then, too? The first time since—"

"Yes. I wouldn't have been so forward otherwise. I mean, when I was vamping you then, and also just now at the front door."

They looked at each other silently for a long moment, their mutual melting gaze speaking volumes without words.

But then Kefildur spoke up abruptly. "I want to make one thing clear," they said.

"Please do."

"While I used the portal in the Tour des Corbeaux specifically to amaze you with my unexpected appearance, I've never used that other world to help me break and enter on an actual job. It doesn't seem fair to the other thieves, somehow. And anyway portals are quite rare around Lutèce."

That engaged Janvier's rational brain again. "But you're someone who can change or even lose your shape at will. That explains all those marvelous locked-room mysteries that baffled poor Commissaire Renault."

"Oh! I want to meet him sometime. But yes. I can pour myself through a grating, or flow through a crack under a door, though it takes me quite a while to reassemble myself afterward. All these different kinds of tissue, bones, joints, and everything. You're all so complicated! But that's my birthright. And it's not as if I'm the only elemental ever to visit the city. My capabilities are well known. So I don't think of that as cheating. Anyway, I can't get a painting out of a gallery without carrying it like a human would do, or penetrate a vault without using my hands, either."

"Indeed," Janvier said. "Your skill in either of your vocations would be admirable enough; combined they take my breath away. But now I'm confused about the portal in the Tour des Corbeaux. If you used it to appear in the tower, how could it still be there when it came time for you to lead me through it?"

Le Chat Azur's arch tones entered the elemental's voice. Their speech had been noticeably softer and less provocative in their role as courtesan. "My dear commissaire! I never said there's only one portal in that tower."

"There's two?"

"There's another in the wine cellar."

"What?"

"The tower's the only place I've found with two. I wanted to amaze you! And it worked, didn't it?" Kefildur turned serious and their persona reverted from the thief to the courtesan. "But the thing is, I feel like I should have been honest with you even at our first meeting. It's just ..."

"You were afraid. And the glorious time we just had together was still in the future. It's all right. I would have been afraid in your place, too. I am now, for that matter. But knowing that you're le Chat Azur doesn't change what we just shared, how I feel, or anything to do with us."

"Jules! I'm so relieved! I have many things to be afraid of, but worrying about how you'd react to my deception was the worst! I was the happiest and most frightened I've ever been, at the same time, when I saw you at the front door."

More than anything else at that moment Janvier wanted to kiss them, and then he wanted, despite all his recent exertions, to communicate his feelings once again with his body. But he was conscious of the chevalier in his sad state, of the baron who might yet be alive to be rescued, of the terrible problem posed by the other world and the looming threat of the shadow minister. So, he used his mouth for speaking instead.

"My dear! And I was as happy as I've ever been about an hour afterward, coming back from that summit of pleasure in your arms, realizing I'd pleased you as much as you pleased me. I hope you know already there's nothing about you I don't find charming, admirable, and desirable. But you must understand. I need to know the truth about all these terrible things connected to the ruined city. I need to know the truth of what's really going on in this world."

Kefildur replied, "We're so different! It took me years to face this thing honestly, and it was a struggle to get to the point of even talking to you about it, someone I thought I could trust! But I can't back out now. Please ... ask me what you want to know, and I'll tell you if I can."

They walked together through the mansion till they got to the orgy room, and once again Janvier had to resist the urge to do something entirely different than conducting an investigation. He and Kefildur sat down side by side on pink cushions embroidered with plump hearts that looked to Janvier's resensualized mind more like derrières, which made him wonder if Kefildur was thinking about *his* bottom at that moment since they'd been paying so much attention to it recently—With a stern mental twitch he pulled himself back to the serious matter at hand.

"You've been to the other world," Janvier said. "You've explored it. You've been *initiated*. Did you follow the chevalier in? Was that how you learned of the place?"

"Y-Yes. I want to tell you about him first, how we met, because he must seem so awful the way he is now."

"Certainly. He seems to have made a big impression on you."

"I'd just come to Lutèce because I'd heard from another elemental, a sylph, about the Guilde du Plaisir and I wanted to find out what all the fuss was about. The fuss over bodies and sex, I mean. I knew the language and I'd learned to hold my body together without dripping all over the place, and I had a few bits of advice from the sylph who'd visited Lutèce themself long ago.

"Getting on the frontier coach at Montciel wasn't too bad. It's a tiny little place, a saloon, a stage station and a trading post and everyone there was kind to me. But then I got off the stagecoach at the Gare de l'Ouest in the middle of Lutèce and there were all these strange humans, hundreds of them moving all around me, and tall buildings and street-cars and lights and noise and a million things that aren't forest or mountains or streams or little wooden buildings. I was totally dazzled, overwhelmed really, with no idea what to do, and this human came over to me and said, 'May I be of service?' and I knew somehow that everything would be all right."

"That was l'Étranger?"

"Yes. He took me in, taught me what I needed to know about Lutèce and human society, protected me from people until I was ready, showed me around town, and even sponsored me to the guild. He was incredibly patient and kind, and of course I fell in love with him. In his inner self, he's nothing like his public persona. He cultivates a reputation of being only interested in sensation and novelty. But the truth is very different. He's really very sweet when he's well. Nearly as sweet as you!"

Janvier couldn't help reacting to that. "I still don't understand how I can be such a prize for you. Sorry, I know that's pathetic, I'm not begging for compliments. I just don't see why you fell for me like that. Because—"

"Because I started out by having a crush on my imaginary conception of the man who saved the city, and maybe that's an exaggeration, but that's how I felt at the time. I'd just become comfortable here, stopped being afraid of strangers, and realized what a nice place you humans had made for yourselves. I'd joined the League and was having fun with that, too. Would you believe my original idea was to be able to present Armand with artwork I couldn't afford to buy otherwise? That's why I kept the Orgy Triptych. It's here in a locked room, by the way. We can work through all the two person variations! I mean, except the ones for two women."

"When this is over, I promise to offer up my body as a sacrifice to the arts and sciences in attempting the experiment," Janvier said, and Kefildur giggled before continuing.

"But then I came to enjoy the technical challenge, the thrill, pretending to be this bold, suave thief. It's a game, like pretending to be a man or a woman, and it's a fun one, too. But then the murders started. It felt like the world I'd spent so much time trying to enter was falling apart. And you put it back together. So that's the first thing.

"So I was predisposed to want to love you. But then we finally met and I realized that you'd scarred over your heart! And you were so stern and careful in talking with me, and so courteous and kind ... I was simply overcome. I have this attraction to people who need to be loved, you see, and your need was so great ..."

Again, Janvier was going to say something, because he'd never learned to take a compliment, but Kefildur raised their hand.

"That's not all! I took you to that height of pleasure just now, and you pulled me along with you—you can't do that with technique, you know. Or not just with technique. There has to be a real connection. Real affection. When we elementals make love, bodiless in a river or a lake, there's no physical pleasure, you know? It's purely spiritual. But we mingle our waters, we interpenetrate, and we know each other deeply. That's never happened for me before with a human, not even with Armand. Not until now."

"And now I'm yours and you're mine, right? It sounds so trite when I say it."

"But it's true."

•   •   •

Watching them smile goofily at one another, watching them renew that mysterious connection they'd just formed with their bodies using only eye contact, my heart melted and I realized how horrible my intentions for Janvier had been, born of twisted, malignant jealousy and spite as they were. I like to think I would have refrained from the monstrous deed my heart urged in any event, but I can't be sure. And that lack of certainty is why—but I'm getting ahead of myself. Back to the lovers.

•   •   •

The elemental exclaimed, "Oh! I still haven't told you the important part! How I learned about all this ... stuff. I must be trying to avoid it. One day not long after you arrested the Butcher, I was supposed to be with a client all week, but an emergency came up for her and I went home early with the idea of using some of the thievery skills I'd been practicing to surprise Armand. As it happens, it was almost midnight."

Kefildur looked like they needed support, so Janvier put an arm around their shoulders. The elemental patted Janvier's hand and looked at him fondly, then went back to their story.

"I crept into his boudoir where he had fallen asleep with a book in his arms and a little smile on his face. So sweet to see him like that! I was about to wake him with a kiss when suddenly he rose to his feet. And I thought I was being so stealthy! I was standing right there, but then I realized he didn't even see me, like he was sleepwalking, which I'd heard of but never actually seen anyone do before. I didn't know if I should wake him up or not, so I just hovered by his side as he opened the bedroom door, and even though the gaslight was turned up in there it had become strangely dark. He entered the bedroom and walked straight to the wardrobe and opened it up too. It looked to me as if he was about to walk into his wardrobe which was full of clothes and things, so I put a hand on his arm but he didn't wake up. And then I saw it just as I touched him, a rectangle of inky darkness, right there in the wardrobe. Armand shrugged my hand off and walked into the darkness and disappeared. I didn't even think twice. I followed him right away."

Kefildur shook his head. "Then … I wish I had more. But I woke up in the place with the Metropolitain sign that you pointed out. In the ruins of Place Pigalle. It was morning."

"Something rendered you unconscious and transported you there?"

"I realized that eventually. At the time I was terrified! I couldn't understand what had happened. At first, I thought Lutèce itself had been destroyed somehow, till I realized there were things there that weren't in our city. I spent the whole day walking around in a daze. By nightfall I'd wandered near the butte without encountering another living thing, not even a rat or a pigeon. It's then that I saw them, flying towards that strange white building at the summit."

"Night-gaunts," Janvier said. "One of them almost got me the second time I was there."

"Oh, no! I'm so sorry! I should have warned you more clearly about them. But that first night you were so cool and collected I wasn't sure what you were thinking, whether you believed anything I told you or not. I wanted you to get home safely to Lutèce and I told myself I'd find you again in our city later on to talk more. But Armand had a very bad day and I had to stay with him. If I didn't make him, he wouldn't drink anything but brandy anymore."

"Could that have been what happened to you? A night-gaunt carrying you away?"

"I suppose it's possible. But why would a night-gaunt put me down safely without … without trying to harm me?"

"I hate to say it," Janvier said, "but—"

"You don't have to. I was hoping you'd reassure me that Armand isn't a fairy-tale villain, that he didn't tell a night-gaunt to simply transport me where it would have—would have done something horrible to someone else. It's the obvious explanation, but something about it feels wrong to me. I hope that's not just wishful thinking."

"I hope it's wrong too. The sweetheart of a man who protected you when you needed it most doesn't sound like a villain to me. But he *did* go through the portal. And he's been sleeping in a room with a portal every night. Perhaps a kinder explanation is he was forced to go through by some kind of sorcery. Perhaps he even interceded on your behalf that day. And now he's suffering, maybe for some reason connected to the ruined city. But the thing is, we have to find out the truth."

Kefildur sighed. "I know. I've been shying away from it ever since I followed him into the other world. I think he has too. We never sleep together, not overnight, I mean; so I'm never present in his bedroom at midnight, and I've been too afraid of what I might find to intrude. But that's why I made sure to meet you when I learned you were being assigned to guard the baron's tower. To help me find out the truth."

"Good. So we're agreed. But about that ... you said you *found out* I'd been assigned to guard the tower? You didn't leave your calling card there? You didn't arrange somehow for me to be there in the first place?"

"No! I didn't know that! Someone put one of my calling cards there? I sent one to your flat to pique your interest, but I certainly didn't give one to Baron Corbeau. I have a client in the ministry of the interior who I imposed on to tell me about your assignments when I decided to seek your help. But why would I leave a card with the baron when I hadn't yet learned you'd be assigned there? He has nothing worth stealing."

"Oh. This is becoming too complicated for me to work through. I hate to be the one to bring it up, but are you familiar with the shadow minister?"

"I've heard the name, but—are you saying it's a real person?"

"It's beginning to look that way. A mysterious figure with influence over the government and through them, over the police. Suppose they were the one to pull strings to get me assigned to the Tour des Corbeaux, after leaving your calling-card there to prepare the way?"

"I don't know, Jules. This is so convoluted! But I can't explain it, otherwise."

"In any event it looks like whatever that house is in the ruined city that's connected to this one ... it must be the key to something."

"I think so too. That's one reason I wanted you in particular, I mean before I knew you. Because the whole neighborhood is shielded by spells in the other world. Once I got used to what that city was like, I tried to find out for myself what was going on there. But I couldn't get close. And I didn't dare try Armand's wardrobe again."

"I've never heard of a spell that powerful before."

"Neither have I. But it's like the place is under an invisible dome. I was hoping you could crack it."

•　　•　　•

"Chief!" De l'Épée waved from down the street. She was just emerging from another gated townhouse estate. When Janvier beckoned, she hurried to meet them.

"Inspecteur de l'Épée, I'd like you to meet the ondine Kefildur."

The elemental and the inspector bowed and exchanged Enchantées.

"So much has happened in the two hours since we parted, I can't even begin to tell you all of it," Janvier said. "However, M. Kefildur has my complete trust."

De l'Épée looked at Kefildur with an O of surprise forming on her mouth. They returned her gaze with a smile on their face. Then she looked at Janvier as if to ask a question but changed her mind and turned back to the elemental.

"It's an honor to meet such a famous celebrity," she said. "May I compliment you on your exquisite choice of skin color? Such a beautiful azure!"

"Why, thank you!" Kefildur exclaimed. "Yours is quite nice, too."

Janvier was amused to see de l'Épée's blush. "I don't suppose you know where Frémont is?"

"No sir, not exactly, but I saw him twenty minutes ago some distance up the street and we waved at each other. I expect he can't have gotten very far in that time."

"Come on, then. Let's take a stroll and wait for him."

It was only another fifteen minutes before Frémont emerged from another house to find the three of them waiting for him. His boggle at seeing Kefildur was even more pronounced than de l'Épée's, due to his celebrity crush on the courtesan.

"Before we proceed," Janvier said, "I have to confess something. With M. Kefildur's permission. The fact is I've fallen for them. Since they are also le Chat Azur and are central to our investigation for another reason as well, I'm hopelessly compromised as an officer of the law in this matter. It's my intention to proceed with the investigation regardless, but if you think I've lost my way due to infatuation it's your duty to either bring me up short or report me to Lambert, whichever you think is best."

De l'Épée and Frémont looked at one another.

"You tell him, Jeanne-Marie," Frémont said. "I'm too astonished at this ... coincidence, is it? But I'm also delighted."

"That's it, Chief," de l'Épée said. "We're absolutely delighted for you. You know how highly we esteem you. It's been plain to both of us that you've been, how shall I say it? Pining? In desperate need of a relationship, anyway, someone to take care of you and someone to take care of. We've even discussed strategies for getting you hooked up. But of course, we couldn't broach the subject. I mean, not directly anyway."

Janvier felt he should be blushing violently, should be terribly embarrassed, but instead he felt free and light, like he'd finally put down some heavy weight he'd been carrying around.

"I wish I deserved this esteem. And this affection too, to be honest. But I'll take it. I've learned a great deal just now from M. Kefildur, so if you don't mind, let's walk to the Tour des Corbeaux and I'll tell it all to you to settle it in my head. Kefildur, please fill in anything I missed or forgot."

10

I T TOOK ALMOST THE ENTIRE half-hour's walk to recount even a summary. By then it was late afternoon on Wednesday.

"Right," Janvier said as they approached the Tour des Corbeaux. "I think these are the key points.

"One. Armand l'Étranger is mixed up in this. My sense is he's more of a victim than a prime mover, based on Kefildur's description of his character and the strange events of that one night, but we really don't know for sure what's going on.

"Two. The answer to the question of the chevalier's involvement is likely to be found at the house in the ruined city. No certainty at all. Just likely, right?

"Three. The night-gaunt that carried off Baron Corbeau may have come from that white building atop the other world's Butte de Mars, the one that I saw night-gaunts flying around and from which that one monster in particular was able to attack me. Again, just speculation, but plausible, anyway.

"Four. The shadow minister exists and is either behind or at least involved with some of these events. They may or may not be inimical, but they're definitely pulling some strings, both through official channels and in other ways. In particular it seems they assigned us to Baron Corbeau's case, fabricating a threat with one of le Chat Azur's cards.

"Five. The reason for that ruse may have been because the shadow minister knew the baron was about to be attacked and wanted us in place to deal with the assault, or it may be because they wanted to provoke le Chat Azur to appear. Or both, or neither, I suppose.

"Is there anything I've overlooked?"

De l'Épée raised her hand. "Just a question of priorities. Much as I'd like to find out what's going on in the house in the ruined city, I suppose it's more likely the baron has been transported to the white palace on the butte."

"Agreed. However ... I think it's foolhardy to venture up the butte at night when we know it's haunted by those monsters, especially considering they're apparently not present during the day. I suggest going to the ruined city's version of the house in the 8th first, and then if nothing more urgent has compelled us elsewhere, waiting till after sunrise to climb the butte to the palace."

"Spending a whole 24 hours there? Very good." Frémont sounded unusually businesslike. "I also have a question. I have mixed feelings about the answer, too."

"Go ahead," Janvier said.

"There's one more person in on the secret. And I'd feel better having a powerful sorcerer along with us. It's just ... what we're going to do may be dangerous. I don't mind it for myself. Our motto *is* 'render assistance', after all, and Baron Corbeau is in grave danger if he's still alive, so it's our plain duty to try and rescue him. But I feel bad about suggesting we request a civilian's assistance, and the fact she's your mother makes it even worse."

"I've put some thought into this," Janvier said. "For me the problem is that she really is a superb sorcerer. And combined with the fact she'd never forgive me if we went without her … I'm a little sick about the idea, but I'm inclined to call her."

"I'm for it," de l'Épée said. "I mean … one Janvier is pretty good, but two of them? Absolutely."

•   •   •

If the officers had been more familiar with mortal risk they might well have had different opinions, but even after Janvier's close call with that night-gaunt they found it hard to credit that kind of danger. The vast majority of deaths in Lutèce were due to diseases of extreme old age or to accidents. Not one police officer in the whole history of the force had ever died due to homicide, nor had any ever committed such a ghastly deed, not even in self-defense.

•   •   •

The three officers, Kefildur, and Professeur Janvier had dinner at Aux Deux Verres[5], a bistro in Janvier's neighborhood in the 18th arrondissement, a place he knew he could reserve the back room for a private dinner. Janvier had worried about how his mother would react to the series of revelations he delivered over the course of the meal, and he worried even more about her reaction to Kefildur. But apart from one moment of exquisite but fortunately private embarrassment

---

[5] Kefildur had no real need to eat, but just as they had painstakingly developed the ability to experience erotic sensuality through the various organs and tissues of their simulated body, they had also learned to derive pleasure from the smells, tastes, and textures of food and drink. This esthetic was honed over time under the tutelage of Chevalier l'Étranger, a noted epicure.

For those readers who are interested in such things, they chewed and swallowed their food in the usual way, extracted and absorbed every bit of moisture, and expelled the remainder in the form of small solid cubes of compressed but undigested material.

Whether either their amatory or gustatory senses at all resembled those of the humans they emulated is impossible to determine due to the philosophical principle of privacy, but the superficial evidence of their tastes suggests they enjoyed much the same sensations as humans.

when he made the introduction and he felt from his mother's warm smile that she'd instantly penetrated and apprehended every aspect of their brief relationship, all went smoothly.

She agreed that the chance of saving an innocent victim motivated risks that might otherwise be considered reckless and declared that her interest in the phenomenon of the portal and the nature of the other world was so strong that she would willingly take reckless risks to participate even if there were no victims to save. This didn't entirely reassure Janvier, but he knew that any further objections he might make were essentially emotional and illogical given that he was planning to take the same risks himself.

•　　　•　　　•

They broke up after dinner to make their individual preparations and returned to the Tour des Corbeaux at 11:00 PM. Janvier had brought a day-hiker's small pack with jerky, candy, water, and a medical kit. De l'Épée and Frémont had packs too, while Kefildur was carrying a small satchel. In addition to her own small kit, Professeur Janvier arrived with a lever-action shotgun resting on her shoulder.

"One of my colleagues in the Ordre Écarlate enjoys the punishing hobby of taking long solo hiking trips in the wilderness up north," she said. "She uses this to shoo off any bears or catamounts who might trouble her. I know the police never use weapons, but I thought just in case ..."

"Aren't you a specialist in high-energy sorcery?" Kefildur asked.

"Yes. But that's a more terrible weapon than any firearm. I've never cast a spell meant to harm anyone, and now I'd rather not have to if I can avoid it. And where a cartridge of birdshot might just discourage someone, a blast of magical fire has rather more permanent effects."

•　　　•　　　•

Janvier felt himself growing more and more nervous as midnight approached, but he wasn't alone; all his companions were visibly tense by the time his pocket watch chimed the hour. He ascended the ladder from the tower's eighth floor, the professeur following him just behind, her hand on his ankle to receive the initiation effect, the other three coming immediately after in order to get through the portal before it closed.

He was gratified to hear his ordinarily imperturbable mother's gasp as she noticed the strange gloom surrounding them and the black rectangle of the portal at the ladder's top. They all passed through without incident. Janvier allowed the professeur a decent interval to acclimate herself to the glorious and terrible nebula overhead and to the desolation of the ruined city all around the tower.

"Right," Janvier said after they went downstairs and out into the street. The dead night-gaunt had vanished, an alarming but not urgently threatening development. "It would usually be ten minutes' brisk walk from Place des Lutins to Avenue de Marigny, but with all these blocked and ruined streets it might take half an hour to get to the far side of the 8th."

Their destination was south-southwest, but with some roads blocked off due to rubble fields and building collapses, they had to detour east and southeast several times. Rounding a corner past a mostly standing six-story building, they all stopped short. A ruined baroque theater with a collapsed dome was on the next block. Some of the portico was still standing, and everyone in the party recognized it; this was the palatial home of the Opéra National in Lutèce[6]. The building here looked to be a perfect copy, what was left of it anyway, and it was in the right place in the ruined city, too.

"How is this even possible?" Professeur Janvier asked. "The general similarity of the cities is uncanny enough. But this ... it looks exact. It's not as if the same architect and builders could have carved two columns or two limestone

---

[6] Some foreign readers may know it as the Palais Garnier.

slabs for every one they actually used, and shipped the rest off with the plans to the other city for bird-people to build."

"There are other correspondences," Kefildur said. "The Jardin des Lapins, it's here too, overgrown, but with exactly the same dimensions as in our city. And the presidential palace is a ruin here, but it looks like it was once much the same as ours. One thing, though. Whenever there's a very close match, the thing that's matching is always pre-Palimpsest in our world. Nothing built in Lutèce in the last 500 years is present in this city."

"Ah. Highly significant. But don't ask me to explain it."

De l'Épée and Frémont had been fairly quiet during the journey, content to let the two Janviers say anything necessary. But now de l'Épée pointed and said "Look." A block to the east, a ruined wall six stories high still stood in the midst of a field of rubble. And atop it—

"Night-gaunt," Janvier said. He stared at it for a long moment before he remembered how he'd somehow called the one from the butte the previous night, but this one didn't react to his gaze. At this distance it was a mere silhouette outlined against the eerie blue radiance of the great nebula, but when it shifted its wings there could be no mistaking it for anything man-made. "Either it hasn't noticed us or it doesn't care. Kefildur, what do you know about them?"

"Not much," the ondine said. "I've never seen one perched on a rooftop like that. Flying around the butte, yes, occasionally flying high overhead on some unknown errand. But I'm not an expert on this city; I've only been here for perhaps a week's worth of time, exploring and trying to get past the warded area around the Avenue de Marigny or whatever they call it here."

Frémont had been scanning the area, and now it was his turn. "Another one," he said. "It's in our way, too, right in front of us, not far down the street. Should we avoid it?"

"It must have noticed us if it's paying any attention at all," Janvier said. "I say no. I mean, we have sorcery, a shotgun, and savate on our side, after all. If we start diverting too far, we'll never get anywhere."

The professeur and the elemental hesitated, clearly waiting for the two police officers to weigh in.

"Sounds good," said Frémont, and "I agree," de l'Épée said. "There's something suspicious about their placement, too. I bet we'll see a third one soon."

They walked cautiously past the second night-gaunt, moving within twenty meters of its perch atop a broken lamppost. It plainly saw them (or sensed them without eyes, anyway), because as they passed it by its blank faceless head slowly turned to track them, but it made no other move.

"There's your third," Frémont said, pointing out another creature atop a broken wall. "How did you know?"

"North-north-east to south-south-west. Where does that line go?"

"Oh! From the Butte de Mars to Avenue de Marigny."

"Right. And each one is in line of sight of the next. It's like they're making a chain from one location to the other."

They continued, sighting two more night-gaunts extending the line. Everyone stopped short as the neighborhood of the Avenue de Marigny came into view a few blocks away. It had been invisible before, the two- and three-story mansions of the avenue hidden by some taller buildings that remained more or less intact. But now that they were close, the strange halo Janvier had seen from atop the tower was visible, surrounding the street and its houses like a dome of faintly sparkling energy.

"Ah! Give me a moment, please." Professeur Janvier reached into her bag and produced a brass face-plate with a number of colored lenses mounted on hinged plates; it reminded Janvier of an instrument that he'd had to look through during an eye exam. She peered through the lenses, swapping several in and out over the course of a minute.

"I've never seen such a large and powerful warding spell before." She flipped a green lens into place. "I believe ... it's weakening. Yes. Something is damaging it, or perhaps it's weakening due to not being properly sustained."

"I've tried to get past it several times," Kefildur said. "When you get very close it's like walking through gelatin, and after a while I couldn't move forward at all."

"What's that sound?" Frémont asked.

"What? Oh."

It had been so faint Janvier hadn't noticed until Frémont pointed it out.

"Chirping birds, perhaps? Or frogs? Strange to hear them at this hour, though."

"It sounds like it's coming from up ahead. Let's go see."

They walked past a final night-gaunt, perched atop a mostly intact block of flats much like Janvier's own building. The twittering sound grew louder.

"What's *that*?" De l'Épée whispered.

In front of them at the boundary defined by the sparkling field, a huge blobby thing like a mass of protoplasmic bubbles ten meters across plastered itself against the shimmering surface, trying to penetrate it with pseudopods, spiky tentacles and other appendages that kept forming from its amorphous body and collapsing once again as they flailed at the barrier. Within the creature's body, huge staring eyes appeared in the bubbles and vanished while hundreds of beaked mouths burst through the thing's flesh, emitting the chirping sound they'd heard before: "Tekeli-li! Tekeli-li!"

The sparks in the field damaged the monster's pseudopods as they came in contact, causing bubbles of the creature's tissue to blister and burst. The substance of the warding field looked thinner where the monster had been attacking it.

A wave of revulsion rippled through Janvier's gut at the sight of this creature, a mass of seething flesh forming and reforming its body, wounding itself over and over as it tried to penetrate the ward. His companions were similarly affected, staggering or recoiling from the sight. They'd walked past a broken masonry corner and were about a hundred meters from the monstrosity, in direct line of sight. If those eyes forming in its body could see, it should have noticed them, but it ignored the five companions; all its energy was devoted to attacking the magical barrier.

By mutual accord, no words needing to be spoken, they moved quickly around the perimeter of the ward until they were out of sight of both the monstrosity and the watching night-gaunt. It was hard to see clearly through the sparkling field in the dark, but it looked to Janvier as if a house very much like Chevalier l'Étranger's was at the center.

"Right," Janvier said, feeling a little better now that the monster was no longer visible. "Let me just say what this looks like. That monster is trying to batter its way through the warding spell. A night-gaunt is watching it, the end of a chain that seems to be connected to the butte. We don't know for sure what's going on, but it certainly looks like someone or something at the butte is commanding the monster through this chain."

"That's what I think, too," said de l'Épée. "I know we can't be sure about people and purposes here, and I hate to rush to judgment on looks alone, but it's hard for me to believe that whoever's behind that thing is benevolent."

"Agreed," Janvier said. "Mother, do you think we can get through this field without destroying it? Without letting that monster in too?"

"Let's try an experiment. Jules, would you mind approaching the boundary? I want to see how it reacts." She produced her lensatic mask again and held it up to her face.

Janvier took a few cautious steps toward the edge of the field. The radiating sparks seemed to be bending away from him as he approached.

"Yes. Good. Another step. Now hold out your hand without touching anything."

He was only a step away now. Janvier raised his hand and the sparkles of light flew away in all directions.

"Good. Now withdraw."

Janvier retreated slowly. When he was four meters away the field resumed its former appearance.

"As far as I can tell," his mother said, "your presence is repelling the field, not damaging or annihilating it. It could be if you just walk forward you'll create a hole or a tunnel through it, but I don't think it will be permanent. The field isn't solid through the interior of the region it's protecting, it's more of a hollow shell, so I think after twenty meters or so it should reform behind you."

"Very well. In some other circumstance, I'd test it alone for safety. But I think we should keep together. Mother?"

"Yes. That seems prudent. I'll keep monitoring as we proceed."

They formed up in a tight group, Professeur Janvier peering through her lenses as they moved forward. Again the sparks fled Janvier's approach, and as he moved toward the surface of the field it bent away from him, forming a dimple and then the beginning of a tunnel through the shimmering spell.

"It seems to be working," he said.

De l'Épée was bringing up the rear. "May I suggest we move faster? That thing has noticed something is happening."

Turning his head, Janvier could see the creature oozing rapidly toward them around the curve of the warding field. It was extending long pseudopods as it moved, coming on much faster than he would have guessed possible for it.

"Run!" Janvier shouted, and they raced forward as fast as they could while staying together.

The tunnel he was forming stayed open to the rear, and Janvier was afraid the creature would soon find its way in as well, but just as its leading pseudopod approached the gap, the sparks from either side closed in once again. From behind he could hear "Tekeli-li! Tekeli-li!" but the creature bounced off the field and it slowly oozed its way back toward its original position.

"That's it," Professeur Janvier said. "We're through."

•   •   •

They approached the center of the space silently. This warded zone felt insulated from the outside world; the frantic attempt at incursion by the monstrosity, horrifying as it had been, was now at a distant remove.

"At last," Kefildur breathed, as they stood outside the mansion's open gate. "At last we'll know the truth."

The structure and its grounds were identical to l'Étranger's Sans Souci in Lutèce, even down to the golden statue of a winged youth in the fountain (a functioning fountain!) outside the front door, and the rows of roses that lined the path. Other estates nearby were dilapidated and abandoned, but Sans Souci was pristine, as if a large staff were maintaining its perfection.

"Well," Janvier said. "No sense just standing out here. Let's go inside."

As Janvier passed through familiar halls with furnishings identical to those in Lutèce, he saw neither servants nor guests. Frémont couldn't help whistling as they entered the orgy chamber. "This place must be something else during the chevalier's nocturnes."

"They're really quite delightful," Kefildur said, smiling at their memories. Then they frowned. "I don't know if we'll ever have another, however."

Finally, they came to the double doors of the boudoir. Janvier felt much the same hesitation as last time, but he knew no other course of action was possible anymore. Really, his biggest fear was that the room would simply be empty, and that this whole fraught and horrifying expedition had been conducted to reach an empty, hollow shell.

"Here we go," he said, and flung open the doors so forcefully they slammed off the walls to either side.

•   •   •

The room was much the same as the one in Lutèce; the main difference was that in this chamber the person inside was reclining on the chaise longue, not sprawled beside it.

"Armand!" Kefildur rushed forward to bend over the recumbent figure. "Wait," they said. "This isn't him ... is it?"

Janvier advanced with the others to see that the person looked like l'Étranger, but an older, wearier, and sicker version of the same man. He appeared to be alive but unresponsive, eyes open but not aware of their presence. As Janvier looked down at the man's face, one of those green eyes seemed to expand until he was a speck adrift in a vast emerald sea, and he fell down through the central pupil into another world.

11

I N THIS NEW WORLD, Janvier was a mere disembodied viewpoint. He was looking into the face of yet another version of Chevalier l'Étranger, this one perhaps seventeen years old. The youth wore an ill-fitting uniform of bluish iron gray, a single chevron on his sleeve, an ugly steel helmet on his head, and a leather pack strapped to his back. He clutched a rifle in his hands.

The chevalier crouched against the wall of a deep trench reinforced with wood beams and sandbags, along with dozens of other similarly dressed men. An ear-splitting cacophony of whistling shrieks and powerful explosions came screaming down from above, shaking the ground. Sprays of mud and fragments of metal rained down on him, dirtying his uniform.

●　　　●　　　●

The people of Lutèce have no words for "war" or "soldier"; the nation has no armed forces or even border guards. The police have never even carried truncheons. They do take some limited martial arts training, for example de l'Épée's savate practice, but for her it was a sport that she never expected to actually make use of as a police officer. Janvier had no cultural or even historical context for what he saw. The action in l'Étranger's vivid memory of Verdun made no sense to him except as a pure nightmare.

•　　•　　•

At length, the sounds of explosions receded into the distance, and someone was shouting "Vite! Commencez l'assaut! La mort ou l'honneur!"

The intention behind this command was so alien that for a moment Janvier didn't recognize it as the language of Lutèce. The chevalier and the others with him scrambled up ladders from the base of the trench and emerged into a blasted, brown wasteland beneath swollen steel-gray clouds. Nothing lived in this waste of mud and craters that seemed to go on forever.

Half a kilometer distant, a wave of annihilation was marching away from the men who had just emerged from the trench, a wall of enormous explosions sending sprays of mud and earth dozens of meters into the air. It seemed nothing could possibly survive that destruction. After marching onward for another half a kilometer, the explosions abruptly ceased, leaving roiling clouds of smoke and a shocking silence in its wake. Along with the young l'Étranger, hundreds of other identically clad men thrashed heavily forward over the muddy, broken ground.

For the first terribly slow hundred meters of progress all seemed well, but then the figures around the man started falling and from the distant sound of rapid fire. Janvier realized people on the far side of the smoke were shooting at these men, hundreds of impacts in the earth testifying to the volume of lead being thrown. Though he couldn't understand why this was happening, Janvier tried to scream within the silence of his own mind, "Take cover!" but to no effect. The men kept running, or rather plodding, each footfall sucked down by the greedy earth and having to be ripped free again. More and more men fell and still they persisted.

And then the explosions began again, not marching away into the distance but right in among the advancing men, blasting bodies and body parts into the air and smashing the few still living with hammering shock waves.

The young chevalier was knocked flat by a near miss, skidding into a crater that was now stained with blood from the destroyed bodies of his companions. His strange green eyes locked wide open, and just like the crater they began to turn red, stained from the inside with blood. He fought to his knees, his lips snarling wide to reveal teeth clenched in a rigid rictus. No words were spoken, but Janvier knew the man was begging desperately for some escape, any way out of this nightmare, though who he should be beseeching was a mystery.

•   •   •

I perhaps should have mentioned this before, but the people of Lutèce have no conception of religion, and no words for anything like prayer, temple, or god, either. When even the most inchoate primitive notions of religion arise, I make sure to stamp them out, to eradicate them utterly. I know no more pernicious principle under heaven than religiosity.

•   •   •

The crater filled with blood, and even in the depths of this horrible vision Janvier knew that was unreasonable, there weren't enough bodies to supply that much blood, but the impossible flow increased, rapidly filling the crater, up to l'Étranger's thighs now, up to his waist, up to his shoulders, his neck, and still the young chevalier didn't move, didn't rise, didn't try to save himself, the blood was covering his face now, rising over his head ...

Everything was red with blood, the whole world was drowned in it, and red was all Janvier could see. Then, writhing through an infinite ocean of swirling blood, a black tentacle pierced the surface and receded, a black tentacle grasping the figure of a man.

•   •   •

"Jules! Jules!"

For a dizzy moment Janvier had no idea where he was, but then he became aware he was in Kefildur's arms, which was such a pleasant place to be it took him another moment to realize he had other things to do than relax in the elemental's embrace. His mother was bending over him, and both Frémont and de l'Épée were looking on anxiously.

"I seem to have suffered a vision," he said. "But I feel all right now. What did you see happen?"

"You collapsed, all of a sudden," Kefildur said. "I barely caught you in time before you hit your head."

He struggled to his feet with the elemental's assistance. "I'm fine," he said. "I really am." Then: "He didn't react at all?" Meaning the figure on the chaise.

"No. We haven't had time to see to him yet."

De l'Épée moved over to the chaise. "The man, the chevalier or whoever he is, seems to be asleep rather than unconscious. But I can't wake him up."

Professeur Janvier studied the recumbent chevalier through her lenses. "Remarkable," she breathed. "Truly astonishing."

"What?"

"He's maintaining the ward himself. Personally. All the power of the spell is coming from him. It should be impossible. No one should be able to supply that much energy over such a large area. And that's not all. There are other magical channels running into and out of him from far-away places. I don't know what they're doing, but it's like he's at the center of a vast network of sorcery. Even Jules' presence is hardly distorting them at all. I've never seen anything like this before."

Kefildur put their hand on the chevalier's forehead and swayed; Janvier rushed forward to prop them up. "You too?" he asked. "A nightmare vision?"

"No! He showed me. Something's coming. From outside. We have to go out there and meet it. If we don't …"

"What? What's coming?"

"I don't know! I just know we have to go! Now!"

Professeur Janvier handed her shotgun to Frémont. "You know how to use this?"

"No!"

"It's easy. Pull this lever to load and cock it. Then brace it against your shoulder, pull the trigger. It's got six shells in the clip."

"But—"

"I'll follow you out. I have something to do here first. Go on!"

The four of them hastened out of the mansion and ran toward the north side of the field where the monster was still attacking it. It was swinging a heavy bulbous pseudopod at the field like a hammer. With each blow the bulb exploded in a burst of steaming fluid and the grievously injured member withdrew rapidly into the creature's body, but a new pseudopod was already forming and repeated the stroke a few seconds later. The field flickered around the point of the blows and a shower of sparks sprayed out. When the pseudopod withdrew the field was visibly dimmer, with fewer glimmering sparks present in its medium.

"What can we possibly do against that thing?" Frémont asked. "It probably wouldn't even notice the shotgun."

Janvier stared numbly at the monstrosity for a moment. Then he turned his head. Yes. The night-gaunt was still perched on its wall-top. "Maybe it's being controlled. We'll have to go outside again. Run with me to the other side, we don't want it cutting us off."

Again, Janvier's presence repelled the ward and formed first a tunnel and then a bubble in the body of the barrier field. This time the monster seemed too preoccupied with its own efforts to notice the disruption around the far side, and so they emerged without interference.

They gave the monstrosity a wide berth and ran around to the base of the night-gaunt's wall, which was around 20 meters off the ground. Frémont worked the lever on the shotgun. He put the gun's butt up against his shoulder, aimed carefully along the barrel. He pulled the trigger and staggered under the recoil.

The sharp report of the gun stretched out into echoes as the sound bounced off the building walls nearby. The night-gaunt was untouched and seemingly uninterested.

"Ouch," Frémont said, rubbing his shoulder. "This thing punches back."

"Here. I'll help you brace." Janvier stood behind him, practically wrapping the younger officer up in his arms. He kept one hand above the butt as Frémont reseated it against his shoulder, stretched out his other arm to provide additional support under the barrel, and then leaned into Frémont's back. "Ready?"

Frémont jacked another round into the shotgun's chamber, aimed again, and pulled the trigger. Janvier felt the recoil communicating through his own body, but this time the packet of shot struck the night-gaunt squarely in the chest, knocking it off its wall.

Janvier was hoping to see the creature topple from its perch and fall to earth like the one atop the baron's tower, but this one managed to right itself in mid-air. If it had been acting under orders it ignored them now, swooping down towards them, wings beating hard.

Frémont pulled the shotgun lever frantically and fired again, but the shot only clipped the night-gaunt's wing, sending it into a tumble that smashed into the two detectives, knocking them down against the dirty broken cobblestones of the street.

Frémont grunted and fell backwards and Janvier's head bounced off a stone. The night-gaunt somersaulted past them several more meters until it bashed against a broken streetlight.

Frémont was laid out on his back while Janvier was on his hands and knees trying to see past the red haze that had descended over his vision. He knew the night-gaunt was rising to its feet and then he saw it clearly, looming over him, clawed hand pulled back for a slash. De l'Épée slammed into it, screaming, both feet extended in a vaulting sacrifice kick to the chest that knocked the creature back so that its head struck the metal streetlight base with a crunching sound. The night-gaunt jerked once and lay still. De l'Épée dropped to the hard stones of the street with a thud, the breath knocked out of her, and so it seemed like an eternity before the three of them managed to scramble to their feet, Kefildur aiding each of them in turn to stand upright.

"You're two for two with night-gaunts," Janvier said, breathing hard.

"Ha," said de l'Épée. "You set it up for me. That was good shooting for a beginner, Frémont."

Frémont groaned and rubbed his shoulder. "I'd just as soon not become an expert. It hurts too much."

"Umm ... Jules ..."

Janvier's gaze followed Kefildur's pointing arm. The monstrosity attacking the field was frenzied now, hundreds of mouths opening and closing in its flesh, screeching out horrid meeping choruses of "Tekeli-li! Tekeli-li!"

Heedless of the damage it was inflicting on itself, the protoplasmic creature launched dozens of pseudopods, tentacles, and spiky barbs from its body, replacing them with new members instantly as they exploded against the field in bursts of steaming fluid. A blast of bilious steam rose up around it, obscuring it from view, and in that moment the whole warding field failed, collapsing in on itself with a hiss and a swirling storm of sparks covering the whole neighborhood it had guarded.

For a few moments no one moved, but then the steam dissipated to reveal the monster, intact, only slightly diminished by its exertions. The thing started oozing forward into the Sans Souci grounds.

Janvier trotted toward the blobby horror, not knowing what he could do but feeling that he needed to do *something*, when a bright glow on the monster's far side made him pause. He circled around to the side to see his mother building a brilliant plasma ball between her outstretched hands, a sorcerous display brighter and more intense than anything he had seen her demonstrate before. The sphere was composed of swirls of red and blue light that swam rapidly around the orb like demented fish, faster and faster. A keening two-tone whine came from the plasma, rising through the scale until it was inaudible except for a teeth-clenching hum that seemed to resonate through Janvier's skull.

The sphere was too intense to look at directly now and the professeur's hands were shaking from the effort required to contain it. The monstrosity had noticed her at last and it oozed forward, extending two pseudopods that it clearly meant to grab or engulf her with.

Professeur Janvier released her sorcery. A coruscating bolt of purple plasma pierced the blobby creature and detonated something deep inside it, releasing a blast so intense that even with his eyes clenched shut a blotchy afterimage interfered with Janvier's vision when he looked to see what had happened. The whole area was full of nauseous-smelling steam, and when it cleared a minute later there was nothing left of the creature at all. In the midst of the dissipating vapor, Professor Janvier knelt on the ground, head bowed.

"Mother!" Janvier raced forward to embrace her before she could collapse altogether.

"That was something, wasn't it?" She relaxed limp in his arms for a moment, which terrified him, but then took a deep breath. "I'm all right now. Help me up, please."

He pulled her to her feet. "What did you do? I've never seen anything like that before!"

"I shouldn't normally have been able to. The power of sorcery is usually limited by a practitioner's individual capacity to summon the requisite forces. But that's why I stayed behind. I tapped one of those etheric channels connected to the chevalier. That did the trick."

"Amazing. I'm proud of you, Maman."

She squeezed his hand. "As I am of you. Just don't ask for an encore. I doubt I'll be able to light a match with sorcery for a week."

"Excellent! Such power would be ... problematic to deal with for the next short while. It's ... just as well you can no longer wield it."

Janvier whipped around to face the source of the voice. Striding through the dissipating cloud of steam came a familiar gaunt figure in a tattered black frock-coat. Great skeletal wings branched from his back now and his pallid face had been flensed away to reveal a bloody skull in whose orbits enormous yellow eyes still glistened, and between whose bony jaws a red darting tongue was still set.

"You killed my shoggoth," said the figure. "It was ... the only one in the world. Though there will be ... more soon, of course ..."

"Baron Corbeau?" Those painful ellipses made it clear to Janvier there was no mistake.

"Not entirely ... not anymore." It was hard to understand his lipless speech.

"Weren't you kidnapped? Carried off by a night-gaunt?"

"Say, rather ... that I was awakened ... to my heritage. Come with me now. It's time to end this ... shadow puppeteer once and for all."

Baron Corbeau started walking forward, toward the Sans Souci mansion. Frémont stepped in front of him. Janvier felt a surge of pride at his inspector's boldness, and fear as well, concerned for what the uncanny baron might be able to do to him.

"I'm sorry, sir," Frémont said. "I'm afraid we can't allow that."

"Who are you ... to forbid *me*? We've ... waited so long ... for his strength to fade. For the wall around the world to crumble. For the ancient powers ... who were expelled ... to return ..."

"I don't understand," Janvier said, which wasn't entirely true, as the baron's words had planted seeds of horrid insight in his mind.

"Do you ... not?" the baron asked. "Then allow me ... to enlighten you." He cackled and waved a bony hand and Janvier's eyes closed and he fell into another hallucinatory world, years, decades and centuries passing before his eyes like the flickering images of a cinema newsreel.

•　　•　　•

Janvier saw a world of bird-people, gracile avian humanoids who had once built a beautiful civilization of their own, but who now lived and died at the will of a terrible power, a power so mighty that reality itself was pliable before its mighty will. This Great One was monstrous, alien, and wholly malevolent. It had journeyed across the cosmic abyss to devour the essence of this rich and delectable world, delighted to find the place utterly vulnerable and defenseless.

For centuries the Great One amused itself by ruling over the avian civilization as an oppressive, evil deity, using and abusing the bird-people for its pleasure, dominating them through sheer force of malice. The Great One's power was so vast it felt no need to prey on its subjects for sustenance; rather it allowed the bird-people to consume themselves in fear, hatred, murder, and war. Other, lesser beings from Outside who followed the Great One like scavengers lurked in the darkness, feeding on their avian victims when the Great One wasn't looking, but not daring to usurp the Great One's privileged position.

Little by little, however, the Great One lost interest in its world, and indeed in existence itself. Sated by aeons of cosmic predation, it lay back in a great underground cavern and let mosses grow to cover its grotesque, bloated body, a pale, bulbous tentacled form a kilometer long entombed in the black earth. It allowed the fungal growths that colonized its rotten flesh to burgeon out of control and gave its weary jaded mind surcease in a sleep so deep it approached oblivion.

The lesser entities from Outside who had been drawn to this rich world like flies to decaying meat were greedy for the Great One's power, but fearful of its remaining flicker of life. The slightest twitch of its dying will could wipe them out of existence. So, they watched and waited and furtively fed off the torment of their bird-people victims, afraid to be the first to approach the Great One's almost-corpse but yearning always for that vast access of power it promised.

They waited too long, however, for one more desperate than they stole the power they desired. On another world, a world of malice and catastrophe but withal some small beauty, a foolish mortal youth gave himself over to his leaders' lies and marched off to war. On his first assault in the human abattoir called Verdun, the young man was on the verge of a pointless, futile death when the keening outcry of his tortured soul burst through a crack in the weak walls of his world, and his call for help reached the ears of the dying Great One. Finding the young man's plight deliciously plangent, the tiny velleity of mind that was all the Great One had left was barely enough to pull the youth between worlds, and as the young man fell into the Great One's gaping maw, the elder god's last spark of volition ... guttered out. And that vast reservoir of power, that monstrous but supine intelligence, that limitless Instrumentality that all the lesser powers had been fearful of and hungry for ... passed by a cosmic fluke into mortal hands.

After the agony of his accession to godlike power had passed, Chevalier l'Étranger looked at his new world and found it a circus of horrors. He methodically exterminated those lesser powers who were too stupid to flee and sealed the walls of the world behind a mighty ward. He collected the scattered and traumatized bird-people survivors and gave them a city from his memories, a place in which they could live in peace, no longer subject to the monstrous cruelty of evil gods from other worlds. Exhausted by his exertions, the young man, now a god in his own right, fell into a deep sleep.

When he awoke generations later, he found that the bird-people had multiplied their numbers but were now in the midst of destroying themselves in a suicidal civil war, a dozen deranged plumage factions flailing at one another, the beautiful city he had given them laid waste and almost destroyed. The bird-people's psyches had been so devastated by thousands of years of torment and predation that their culture had acquired an essential insanity, and despite the easy lives the sleeper had granted them they were unable to live in peace.

The young man wept and tried again. He knew that having assumed responsibility for these people, their failures were his fault. He wiped the memories of the bird-people and transformed them into humans, partly because he wanted true companions, partly because he thought he understood humans and would be able to do a better job of providing them with lives of satisfaction and contentment. And so, he instilled in their memories his own recollections of the culture of his birth city, purified and cleansed of the many malicious and distorted elements he'd always despised.

The apotheosized chevalier built a second city in a shadow world into which he poured almost all his power, so that the shadow became substance and the beautiful dream of Lutèce took precedence over the blighted world whose people he had failed. He gave each of the bird-people their own personal back-story, family ties, and living situation within the city. Next, he invented a cultural history for the transformed bird-people, only to wipe it clean in the Palimpsest Event because even his enormous power couldn't provide a true sense of continuity for all these displaced, tormented refugees. His wards awakened in a state of sleepwalking torpor that took a whole generation to fade, wakened to a pristine new city that was nevertheless familiar to their dull, false memories, a city of order and peace, prosperity and pleasure, magic and romance. It was only in the next generation that the citizens of Lutèce awoke fully and began to live proper lives in their old-seeming city that in truth had only been created twenty years before.

Then l'Étranger created a shadow self, an echo of his soul filling a new mortal body so that while he slept in his throne of power, recovering over the centuries from the dreadful exertions of godhood, he could at the same time enjoy the fruits of his creation, dreaming the pleasures he had yearned for as a youth, enjoying wealth, celebrity, and luxury.

The dreaming chevalier, living life after life vicariously through the succession of mortal shadows he cast off for his pleasure, worried that without guidance his protégés might go astray once more. And so he empowered his double to wield subtle power over their government through a myth communicated to their leaders, the myth of the shadow minister.

But what he didn't know was that during his purge of the lesser powers from Outside, some of those vicious alien demigods had in their terror broken off fragments of their psyches. They hid their fragmentary selves deep in the souls of their bird-people prey to be passed on from generation to generation, biding their time until their chance to seize power would at last come again.

He also didn't realize that in his somnolent disregard, greater powers from Outside would be attracted by his world's wealth to burrow into and slowly erode the walls he had erected; that over time the weak spots would show and the shriveled sleeping souls of ancient malice would be emboldened by subtle energies passed to them from Outside. He was unaware that in a time of trouble and terror, when his mortal shadow was crippled by an incursion of cosmic malice into his beautiful city, when the dreaming god himself was placed under siege by intrusions from Outside, one of those transformed bird-people would at last awaken to their true power and march on the sleeping chevalier's seat to devour him and take the world's reins into his own greedy hands.

•   •   •

Janvier broke the surface of the newsreel dream like a breaching whale. Bird-people, he thought dizzily. I'm a bird-person! But where are my wings? And what color is my plumage? For a moment he almost drifted off into a fantasy of flight (or was it a memory of a past life?) but then he remembered who and what he was and he forced his eyes open to see his companions along with the hideous thing the Baron Corbeau had become, standing around the chevalier's chaise longue. The other officers and Professeur Janvier appeared to be asleep on their feet, but Kefildur was shaking their head, and like Janvier himself seemed to be on the verge of reawakening. Janvier thought: *Aren't I supposed to be immune to sorcery? What just happened?* He tried to take a step forward, but he found he was all but paralyzed; he was able to stand, but something was preventing him from moving.

The baron caressed the sleeping chevalier's cheek with the back of his clawlike hand, aping precisely the gesture Kefildur had used with Janvier on their recent encounter. He muttered, "At last ... the stars are right ... the walls of the world will shatter and crumble ... my brethren will flock to my service ... and the kingdom of chaos will come again ..."

"Not if I can stop you," Kefildur said, and he reached out for the baron's neck, an action that would not only have been the elemental's first ever act of violence, but the first ever recorded of any elemental, ever. By the contortion of his face Janvier could see the anguish this deed cost his lover.

"Too late," said Baron Corbeau. He gestured and a brilliant lance of plasma blasted through the elemental's body. Kefildur fell to the floor, his body rapidly liquefying, collapsing into a pool of water at the baron's feet. Janvier felt like his heart had been pierced along with Kefildur's. An icy coldness welled up inside him, desolation mixed with anguish, but he still couldn't move or speak. Baron Corbeau tried to laugh, but something must have been wrong with his throat because he could only produce a horrible rattling caw.

At last the baron recovered. He gestured grandly to his little audience. "Down to four. Alas ... I've already ... seized control of some of the shadow sorceries. Soon the whole power of the Great One ... will be mine ..."

The word "sorceries" triggered something in Janvier's grief-stricken mind. Sorcery. He was supposed to be resistant to sorcery. Why was he still paralyzed? Why had he been so easily dragged along like a puppet to witness all this?

Even passing through the chevalier's warding field he'd never attempted to actively exploit the power of his disability. But now he tried, though he had no idea what he was doing. Janvier had heard his mother explaining that l'Étranger was the center of a network of magical channels, no doubt the resources of that vast Instrumentality he'd inherited from the Great One so long ago. The baron must have seized control of one or more of those channels, just as his mother had—

The room turned dark, and electric chills rippled down Janvier's spine. He saw them then, those channels of power, one of them writhing into the baron's body, worming its way into the base of his throat. Lesser networks of power surrounded each of the four survivors, no doubt communicating the effects of the paralysis and control spells that had been afflicting them. It seemed so easy to pinch off the energy flow that was feeding Janvier's own spell, so he did it and all at once he was free.

"Now ..." said the baron, lowering his hands to the sleeping chevalier's neck. Janvier stepped behind him and wrapped him up in a bear-hug. All the channels of magic connected to Baron Corbeau were cut off at that moment. Released from their own spells, the two officers and Janvier's mother staggered and fell to the floor.

Meanwhile the baron screamed, or rather cawed, a

tortured raven shrieking and struggling to free himself. Even before his transformation, Baron Corbeau had been gaunt and frail-looking, but now he was a fragile thing with hollow limbs, far lighter and more delicate than a night-gaunt, and with none of a night-gaunt's hideous otherworldly strength.

Though Janvier was only holding the baron immobile, the baron's frame had become as brittle as chalk, and as he struggled to free himself Janvier heard the terrible sound of the baron's bones shattering in his arms. The demented creature raved and fought, breaking bone after bone in its frenzy and at last it fell limp, lifeless, and dead.

He let the baron's broken corpse fall to the floor. The shock of this pathetic death at his own hands was too much for Janvier. Darkness rose up around him, and he too felt himself falling.

•　　•　　•

"Thank heaven you survived!" Those were the first words Janvier heard on waking up. He found himself frozen in a colorless instant, his gaze fixed on the ceiling above his head. He was still lying on the floor where he'd fallen Janvier recalled the last time he'd been suspended in time for a conversation. It seemed his memory of that incident had been restored. For a moment he was angry, but then he remembered Kefildur and desolation enfolded him once again.

For the sake of saying anything at all, he asked, "Heaven? What's that?"

"Oh … an outmoded concept. Forget it." The voice was the chevalier's, pleased and self-satisfied as ever. "You have my thanks, my literal undying thanks I should say, for the crucial role you played in this fiasco. It's all my fault of course. Letting these shadow selves scramble around on their own turns out not to have been quite the clever idea I thought when I went to sleep."

Janvier had no response. It occurred to him a lot of what l'Étranger had to say left him flat.

"I'm sorry you had to go through that terrible scene with Baron Corbeau," the chevalier continued. "Would you like me to wipe your memory of it?"

The offer was insidiously appealing. What Janvier wanted right now was first, time and space to grieve for Kefildur, and second to lay down somewhere and go to sleep, hoping that somehow everything would have fixed itself when he awoke, and everything would be back to normal. The chevalier's offer seemed very appealing for a moment. But Janvier knew he had a responsibility, to his people and also to his city.

"I think not," Janvier said. "But what are you going to do? I mean, to me and my mother and my officers."

"Oh, nothing dire. I'll put you back in Lutèce when this conversation is over, back in my shadow's boudoir. You'll find him recovered from his melancholy fits, too; while dreaming, I allowed him to succumb to the same otherworldly influx of malice and alienation that infected that monster the Butcher. The shadow keeps me sane, you see, or rather, he was meant to, but it seems I neglected to protect him properly."

"He lives for you? That sounds horrible. At least for him."

"Oh, he doesn't mind. He's me, you see. I'd love to be in his place. He lives his self-indulgent, hedonistic life, and every so often I call him back to me and we merge so I can experience his memories. That's what Kefildur noticed that night, how they first found their way to this world."

"I see. Why didn't you wipe *their* memory? Why did you let them go free to explore the ruined city?"

"Call it ... sentiment? Ethics? Whatever you like. I was mostly asleep, you understand, so my own reasoning is a bit murky in retrospect. I think I wanted a companion. Someone to share all these secrets with. And now I have you. Ironic."

Janvier let that last remark pass. "I also don't understand why you let the baron go free. Why didn't the all-seeing shadow minister realize what was happening?"

"Ah. Yes. This is embarrassing, but I'm afraid omniscience is rather trying. Even a brief period engaged with the Great

One's Instrumentality is torture for a mere human like me. And then afterward it takes me forever to recover. While I'm dreaming, I'm only aware of the things that catch my interest. And that's mostly been Kefildur, and more recently, you. I did get a sort of twinge about the baron recently, and I thought it might be a good idea to set you on him, but I really had no idea he was about to be … coopted like that."

Coopted! As mild-mannered as he was in normal times, Janvier wished he was standing across from the chevalier in person so he could slap the man's face. All this secretive behind-the-scenes manipulation had caused untold pain. And killed the only person he thought he might ever love.

"This is all your fault, then. Everything, the baron, Kefildur, all of it!"

"I'm afraid so. I acknowledge it, you see? It would have been even a worse failure than the first time around, with those poor bird-people."

"Bird-people like me. Like everyone in Lutèce!"

"Well, yes. Originally. Not that there's anything wrong with that. Your heritage is sounder than mine, anyway; my people used to slaughter one another without even having an elder god as an excuse. For all I know they still do. But now you know more or less everything. So, seeing as you're in this unique position, the only person to ever share all these secrets, I have an offer for you."

In spite of himself, Janvier was intrigued.

"Go ahead."

"I'm willing to cede all decision-making authority regarding this incident. Honestly, I screwed things up too badly to be allowed to decide what to do next. Everything will be up to you, to hide or reveal, publicize or keep secret. My existence, my identity, what happened with the baron, even the nature of the horrors waiting outside the walls of the world for my defenses to weaken. If necessary, the shadow minister will use his influence to protect you from official retribution. You can drag my beautiful city down to hell by sharing your secret knowledge, or let the people live their lives happily and ignorantly as they do now. It'll be completely up to you."

"What's hell?"

"I—you know, Janvier, it's just as well I don't explain it. As useless a concept as heaven. It's something from that world I came from. Verdun, you know? Let's say that was hell."

Janvier paused to consider. Not that he was used to this kind of weird mental speech, but he thought the chevalier was sincere. Well, as sincere as was reasonably possible for a man who had become a god, anyway. And he thought the man was honestly contrite, too.

"Very well," he said at last. "But I don't see why I should be able to make better decisions than you. And you know my bias already. I'm in favor of truth and kindness and all the principles you established for us as ideals in Lutèce. I'll have to think about it. What would we do with this knowledge? How would we react to the understanding we've been the playthings of greater powers all these years? I don't know. I can see why you wanted to suppress the knowledge. It's terrifying."

"Yes. I haven't stopped being frightened in the thousand years since Verdun. It's only in my shadow lives that I'm happy. And in all that time, all those parties, all those orgies, all those pleasures, only one person has ever truly loved me."

"Kefildur." Janvier almost couldn't bear to say their name. He thought it was just as well he was caught in this bodiless, frozen instant, because otherwise he would have broken down in tears, or else—he didn't know what else.

"Yes," the chevalier said. "I didn't even mean to create the elementals, you know. They just sort of sprang up from nowhere when I patterned all the power required to enable human sorcery. And yet, without that one foolish water elemental's love, I think neither of us would have survived. I sowed the seeds of my own ruin, and I would have taken you with me, too."

Janvier would have shaken his head if he could. "I'm not sure I understand."

"Just as well," the chevalier said. "The point is, you won the love of the only person who's ever loved me. Can you even understand how angry that made me? While dreaming, I looked for you, and I found you two on my shadow's lawn. I was on the verge of annihilating you utterly … and then I saw how happy they were, how much Kefildur cared about you … I couldn't do it."

"That makes no sense to me. I could understand sorrow, if they had abandoned you, but they didn't! They were willing to sacrifice everything to save you. Why would you be angry? Don't you—didn't you love them too? Didn't you want them to be happy?"

"I did. I do. And you have no idea how pleased I am to hear you say that. Where I come from, jealousy was almost universal. We were taught that to love was to possess, to dominate, to control … Intellectually these things sickened me, even when I was a young man back in my native Paris, but emotionally … I fear it's baked in. Too late for me to change. You, though, and your people—"

"Us bird-people. Wingless bird-people."

The chevalier chuckled. "Indeed. I see that's still troubling you. I'm afraid they'd already evolved to be too heavy to fly, but I suppose gliding was nice for them, and I took that away. If you like I can grow you some wings and hollow your bones next time you visit and you can try them out."

"I … I can't even comprehend how much power you have. It's really horrifying."

"Yes. I agree. But on the other hand, without it we'd all be dead or else we'd wish we were. Some of the powers that travel between the worlds are far worse than the pathetic Baron Corbeau. If the Great One who called me here hadn't been so old and senile, it would have devoured this world's heart and moved on to its next feast, leaving only a husk behind. There would have been no survivors at all."

"I suppose I should thank you for protecting us from them."

"You're welcome. That's what I meant last time when I said I'd sworn an oath to defend Lutèce. But about the wings and feathers, really, for all practical purposes you're as human as me, and indeed, your bird-people ancestors and my people are so close as to be indistinguishable to something like the Great One, or to the power that awakened in Baron Corbeau. Anyway, whether your kind and generous sensibility is due to your heritage or to my guidance, the fact that you wouldn't have been jealous in my place ... it makes me very happy. You have no idea how delighted I am, now that I'm fully awake. I know how vile that way of thinking is, even if I can't quite free myself of it."

Janvier was silent for a time, thinking about this.

He said at last, "Kefildur. They're so pure. They loved us both. I don't know why, either. I know I didn't do anything to merit it. They just did. But you're a—a whatever you are. You have all this power. Can't you bring them back?"

"Bring them back?"

"Yes. I'd give anything. I'd give my own life if I could."

Janvier was expecting to hear the chevalier say no, perhaps sadly, perhaps flatly. He knew that some things were beyond even the Great One's power. But he wasn't expecting l'Étranger to laugh.

"Oh! Oh! I'm so sorry! It's just—I didn't realize. I thought you knew!"

The shadow minister's hilarity seemed grotesquely out of place, and Janvier was going to answer angrily, but l'Étranger continued, "Look, we're frozen in time now, you don't have to stay stuck in your body if you don't want to. Look down at yourself on the floor, tell me what you see."

All this time, or no-time or whatever it was, Janvier had been ignoring the room and his viewpoint because of the conversation he'd been focused on. The blank expanse of the ceiling he'd been gazing up at didn't seem worth looking at. But now, returning his attention to his frozen senses, with an effort of will Janvier swiveled his gaze around like he was operating a motion-picture camera and looked down at himself, looking himself right in the eyes. Janvier thought his slack, apparently unconscious face looked particularly stupid in this frozen instant, but then he realized he wasn't quite flat on the ground, and when he pulled back a little to see why he saw that rising from the puddle of water that was all that was left of Kefildur, two translucent liquid arms had extended themselves to cradle his head and neck.

"Oh," he said, and the rush of joy he felt was so intense he couldn't speak for a moment.

"Yes. It's quite difficult to kill an elemental. I daresay Baron Corbeau would have found a way eventually, but as it is—Oh, bother. There's no way you can concentrate on this conversation now, is there? We'll have to pick it up again later."

·   ·   ·

The five companions stood on the sidewalk outside of Chevalier l'Étranger's placid townhome estate on Avenue de Marigny in Janvier's native Lutèce. Kefildur had put themself back together physically and the others had more or less accomplished the same trick mentally.

"All's well that ends well, right chief?" Frémont grinned. "I mean, the good guys won, the bad guy lost. Sure, some of it was pretty horrible, but nothing bad really happened in the end. Case closed, right?"

"Not yet," Janvier said. "There are still plenty of loose ends to wrap up. The baron's estate has to be put through probate, and who do you think will be asked to perform the heir search? Our semi-official investigations into le Chat Azur's faked-up theft warning and the baron's break-in and disappearance have to be resolved. The paperwork will probably be horrendous seeing as we'll never find the corpse or a culprit. I'll have to deal with Lambert somehow, too; I'm sure he won't forget how de l'Épée and I jerked him around."

"Oh." Frémont looked crestfallen.

"But that's just trivialities. Back in the other Lutèce, there's the question of that palace on the butte we never did get around to looking into. The chevalier said it was originally a sort of official institution for paying respect to a fictional person, he called it Sacré-Cœur de Montmartre. Cœur, all right, some kind of heart, and Montmartre might be another name for the Butte de Mars. But that strange word, Sacré, he refused to explain, and it's nagging at me. He says it's a blind spot for him now. I think we'll have to look into it when we've recovered from this last little incursion."

De l'Épée asked, "Do we even have time to recover? What if whatever's in the … the Sacré-Cœur tries to do something else?"

"L'Étranger told me not to worry. Whatever it is, if there's anything at all, is trapped in there, and no longer has even indirect access to any of his power. He says he's already dealt with the night-gaunts in the ruined city. But the place is still inaccessible to him so we'll have to deal with it … eventually."

"I see."

"You and Frémont are under official orders to take at least a couple of days off, and if you need more—I'm pretty sure I do—consider them granted in advance. I can't tell my mother what to do but that's my advice for her too."

Professeur Janvier smiled. "The tenured holder of the Ambrose chair in magical studies at the Université de Lutèce and a Magister Exonéré of the Ordre Écarlate can take all the time off she wants."

"How much time will she *actually* take off?"

"Oh … at least half a day. There's a film I've been wanting to see. But those magical channels we found … no one asked me not to try to duplicate them, you know. And then there's the portals, that mysterious darkness, some new insights into a certain commissaire's unfortunate condition … enough to keep me busy for quite a while."

The five companions exchanged embraces, kissed each others' cheeks, agreed to a dinner at Aux Deux Verres on the weekend, and parted company. Or rather, three of them did. Janvier and Kefildur were left together. Both were content simply to look at one another for quite some time. But then they both started speaking at once.

"I was so frightened—"

"I thought you were—"

Neither wanted to interrupt, so they both paused. Each raised a hand to the other's cheek. After another long moment they kissed and all their fear and joy and affection and apprehension passed back and forth wordlessly between their lips until they both broke off at once, conscious that an elderly page wheeling a wire-frame shopping cart full of items from the épicerie down the street had paused, waiting for them to clear the sidewalk.

"Oh no," said the page. "Carry on. This is the city of love, after all."

"We really should find a better place," said Janvier, when they'd apologized and convinced the page to pass them by.

"Le Chat Azur has an absolutely gorgeous hideout in a warehouse basement just across the Serpentine in the 6th," said the elemental. "And Kefildur has a lovely flat close by the Jardin des Lapins in the 1st. Every modern convenience, étage noble, tout de luxe."

"Anywhere you choose to live would delight me," said Janvier. "And I hope to spend as much time as you will allow in both places. But may I offer my own flat as an alternative, just this once? Inferior in charm and luxury to both your homes, I'm sure, but it does feature a concierge who is an emeritus of your guild and a fan of your league, and whose day would be made if you granted him a minute of your time."

"Absolutely!" Kefildur was enthusiastic. "I always like to please my fans."

"I'm a fan too, you know."

"Oh, indeed. One has a civic obligation, after all." Le Chat Azur's arch tones entered the elemental's voice. "One doesn't want to frustrate the police too badly. I understand that despite the annoyances they offer to cat-burglars they sometimes provide quite useful service to the community."

"Just so. Perhaps you'd like to attend a private presentation of the services we offer? We have a wide selection, you see. Not to compete with the Guild du Plaisir, of course, but we like to think we offer satisfaction."

"Nothing sounds better to me," said Kefildur, bowing formally, "than to have a commissaire of the Police Judiciaire at my service. I've always wanted one! It's like a dream come true."

Janvier bowed in turn. He offered his lover his hand and together they strode off down the avenue. Heading home.

•   •   •

This is my envoi. I trust you figured out who the intrusive narrator was early on; I didn't try to hide my identity, after all. At this point I honestly don't know what Janvier is going to decide. I imagine it will be something prudent and sensible and considerate, however, because that's his nature. All's well that ends well, so they say, but this hasn't ended yet, not for any of us. For now though, I remain the shadow minister, watching over the most delightful city in any world while my mortal double does his best to enjoy the city's bounty. Which may or may not include a certain water elemental's favors if they can tear themselves away from their other love from time to time.

Bonne nuit et au revoir.

Oh! One more thing. If this narrative reaches you on one of the far-distant worlds to which I send it, including the benighted planet of my birth, remember, you'll always be welcome in my beautiful city of light.

ABOUT THE AUTHOR

Laurence Raphael Brothers is a writer and a technologist with five patents and a background in AI and Internet R&D. He has published over 40 short stories in such magazines as *Nature*, *PodCastle*, and *Galaxy's Edge*. His noir urban fantasy novellas *The Demons of Wall Street*, *The Demons of the Square Mile*, and *The Demons of Chiyoda* are available from Mirror World Publishing.

ALSO BY THE AUTHOR

THE WORLD'S SHATTERED SHELL

Laurence Raphael Brothers

It's the end of the Age of Kali and our world is dying, its bounds shrunken to encompass a single city.

YOU MIGHT ALSO ENJOY

BLOOD BENEATH THE SAND
Evan Davies

Devlin Narre is a wizard, a sleuth, and a killer for hire — all to varying degrees of competence and consent.

ENLIGHTENMENT
Bruce Golden

When a boy's family is killed, and his home destroyed by marauders, he begins a journey with a traveling old man.

PROPHECY OF HONOR
Fred Waiss

A hundred years ago, an old man staggered out of the desert and found succor at Honor Keep.

www.ingramcontent.com/pod-product-compliance
Lightning Source LLC
Chambersburg PA
CBHW020808310726
48969CB00002B/748